I0640965

Firebrand Firestorm

The Ancestors of Bjorn Esterday

Volume 06

Seek and Find

March, April, May 1776

Wynter Sommers

Published by Pure Force Enterprises, Inc.
California, USA
Since 2002

INGRAM
INGRAM® Distribution

ISBN-13: 978-1-7184-0018-4
ISBN-10: 1-7184-0018-7

DEDICATION

To those who feel strongly about truth,
justice, and the integrity of America;
your honorable actions make us proud.
To those who wonder if their daily
choices matter; your small decisions
impact generations to come.
To those everyday people who don't think
they have what it takes; when you strive
for extraordinary things, the impossible
becomes reality.
Your dreams today become our future
tomorrow.
Thank you for everything you do.

Bjorn Esterday
Was Not Born Yesterday
Series

Firebrand (15 Volumes+Conversation Station Book)
Edges (9 Stories +Conversation Station Book)
Gone (18 Stories + Conversation Station Book)

Bjorn EDGES Series
EDGES Book 1-Swift Encounter
EDGES Book 2-Rousing Attack
EDGES Book 3-One Foot Under
EDGES Book 4-Earthshake
EDGES Book 5-Broken String
EDGES Book 6-Key Witness
EDGES Book 7-Who is She?
EDGES Book 8-Vanish
EDGES Book 9-Chase or Die

Bjorn Series Alternate Reading Plan

1st	Edges Book 1		22nd	Gone Book 10
2nd	Edges Book 2		23rd	Firebrand Vol 9
3rd	Gone Book 1		24rd	Gone Book 11
4th	Firebrand Vol 1		25th	Firebrand Vol 10
5th	Edges Book 3		26th	Gone Book 12
6th	Firebrand Vol 2		27th	Gone Book 13
7th	Gone Book 2		28th	Firebrand Vol 11
8th	Gone Book 3		29th	Gone Book 14
9th	Firebrand Vol 3		30th	Firebrand Vol 12
10th	Gone Book 4		31st	Gone Book 15
11th	Firebrand Vol 4		32nd	Firebrand Vol 13
12th	Gone Book 5		33rd	Gone Book 16
13th	Gone Book 6		34th	Firebrand Vol 14
14th	Edges Book 4		35th	Gone Book 17
15th	Firebrand Vol 5		36th	Firebrand Vol15 (End)
16th	Gone Book 7		37th	Gone Book 18 (End)
17th	Firebrand Vol 6		38th	Edges Book 5
18th	Gone Book 8		39th	Edges Book 6
19th	Firebrand Vol 7		40th	Edges Book 7
20th	Gone Book 9		41st	Edges Book 8
21st	Firebrand Vol 8		42nd	Edges Book 9(End)

ACKNOWLEDGMENTS

We acknowledge those who actively build peace. We acknowledge all the selfless talent which contributed to creating meaningful tokens of consideration and sharing. We acknowledge that every person has a daily choice of right or wrong... and we thank you for choosing the right, good, honorable path filled with integrity because that is the difficult and brave path. Small choices today become lasting monuments of loving hope tomorrow.

CONTENTS

0 PREFACE

As the Jane explores, and Polly settles in, Bryce Aiden Tyler has an epiphany. Meanwhile, those of the servant class navigate new territories to make lasting changes beyond their comprehension. Silversmith, Simms, and others adjust gracefully to challenges they never imagined.

.

1 CHAPTER 48: (APRIL 1776) After the Opera Performance

Lady Sarah Wilson's drawing room had been converted into a theater with mis-match chairs placed in neat rows. All chairs stood facing the piano in an area where the main attraction was to perform. He was, of course, the famous opera singer. Jane's deceased uncle Floyd had been invited to attend this very presentation by the world renown *primo uomo* Sir Henry Mossop.

Jane doubted that he was actually a "sir", just as she doubted "Lady Sarah Wilson" was no more than a self-appointed lady. How gauche it was to loudly proclaim to the world your own attributes, Jane thought. But, she smiled and feigned enjoying this concert.

On the other side of the room sat Mr. Tweedbottom, the tailor from Jane's village. She had seen him across the table at dinner, earlier. She was hoping to ask him why he was there, but he was not within the distance to hold an appropriate conversation.

Dinner had finished and the evening entertainment was to begin. Jane felt now would be an optimal opportunity to discover why Mr. Tweedbottom was at an event to which her Uncle had been invited. Mr. Tweedbottom could have, but did not contacted Jane to announce he was coming to this affair, even though he was fully aware of Jane's plans to attend in her uncle Floyd's stead.

Jane reasoned to herself that the colonies were too new to each have a proper theatrical stage on which to perform in a proper theater.

But, if a famous singer was going to perform at a private home, wouldn't every person of note be invited? Would that include Mr. Tweedbottom? Jane's Uncle Floyd's business partner, Mr. Bryce Aiden Tyler, was not invited. Else he would have mentioned something. Wouldn't he? Jane wondered if she might have had any of these questions swimming in her head if there was a formal opera house built in each colony.

As the crowd funneled in from the dining room to the drawing room, Jane had sidled up to Mr. Tweedbottom remarking how surprised she was to see him there.

He had a neat reply for her which came so quickly, Jane wondered if he had rehearsed in anticipation of meeting her. He did, after all, not allow Jane to finish her question, yet he had a full reply to her unasked question already prepared to roll off his tongue.

Mr. Tweedbottom had explained to Jane, "Nearly everybody had been invited, you know, since there are no formal opera houses built in the colonies."

"Nearly everyone? Then, why," Jane replied with a soft challenge, "is Mr. Tyler not here?"

"Oh! Fiddle!" Mr. Tweedbottom had dismissed, "Bryce Aiden Tyler is a cretin, lacking culture. He cannot be trusted to even behave properly in as refined a setting, as this estate. Mr. Tyler wouldn't appreciate the vocal performance of our famous Sir Henry Mossop."

"Our?' Jane replied.

Conveniently, Mr. Tweedbottom had recognized somebody whom he had to urgently greet. Never-mind the fact that most everybody had already met everybody else over the dinner table but moments earlier.

He quickly excused himself and scurried to the other side of the room, abandoning Jane, who took a deep breath, forced a smile and looked around to decide what her next course of action should be.

Jane searched for a single seat and found one.

Jane situated herself at the end of a row, making polite chit-chat with those around her.

Lady Sarah Wilson now strolled to the front of the room and rang a silver bell to get the audience's attention.

Lady Sarah announced, "If I may, ladies and gentlemen, it is with great pleasure I would like to welcome a gentle Irish soul, who has recently been spending time in our beloved England and has finally arrived to provide us all with the rich refinement we are so starved for in these colonies. May I introduce you to our very own primo uomo, Sir Henry Mossop." She turned to the opera singer and said, "Please grace us with your selections for voice."

Lady Sarah Wilson stepped away to sit

in an overstuffed chair off to the side. Henry Mossop absorbed the eager applause and commenced his performance, which was rife with wild gesticulations and imaginary partners to which he was addressing his arias. The audience reaction only fed the singer Mossop to perform even more dramatically.

The chair Jane sat in was a bit wobbly, due to one leg being a different length from the other three.

She tried to not thump on the wooden floor as she shifted in her seat, yet she found it necessary to adjust her position to provide some comfort. Sensing the beat of the music, Jane timed her chair adjustments to the rhythm of the piano forte, so nobody noticed.

At the end of the long performance, Jane was the first to stand to lead a standing ovation, but the others didn't realize she was simply in an uncomfortable chair.

Comparing Sir Henry Mossop's performance to those she recalled back in London and Milan, Jane felt this "primo uomo" was mediocre at best.

Not only did her late uncle Floyd despise opera, but to subject him to a merely average performance seemed almost cruel. If this were some spectacular performer which may have changed Uncle Floyd's mind, then perhaps Jane could justify why uncle Floyd had been invited, here, but... to be invited to this... this... even in Jane's thoughts she could not come up with a word to describe the performance.

Jane softly said to herself, "Experiencing this would only underscore Uncle Floyd's position about opera in general."

Somebody overheard Jane and commented, "An avid fan?"

Jane smiled not knowing if the question was posed genuinely or in mockery.

"I do appreciate," Jane shared smiling, "the efforts Lady Sarah Wilson has gone through to arrange this entertainment for us. I am not as educated about music as I would like to be. Any thoughts I have on his performance should be received with only minor considerations."

The guest replied, "Yet even thorns are minor slivers which can irritate one's skin, and must be plucked out to obtain relief..."

"Indeed..." Jane smiled. The guest wandered away to converse with another member of the audience.

"Likewise," Jane thought, "I shall seek relief from this tiny annoying thought of mine." Jane wondered why would Uncle Floyd be invited to a distant opera performance by a woman nobody in the Hargreaves household had heard of before.

Jane spied a crowd encircling the celebrity Sir Henry Mossop and felt compelled to join the enthusiasts as they drenched him in a shower of adoring praises for his spectacularly overacted performance.

Mr. Mossop, of course, expected such adoration. "One day, my dears," Henry Mossop announced to his fawning admirers, "There shall be a proper opera house built, and I shall be able to perform on a proper stage, with proper foot lights and enough seats for all of you, my loyal devotees."

There were many questions posed by the titillated crowd, but the one Jane posed gave Mr. Mossop pause.

Jane asked, "Did you make the voyage all the way over to our humble colonies for this performance only or did other business call you here? Our hostess explained you were delayed due to business..."

Henry Mossop did not answer.

Mr. Tweedbottom now made his way to Jane's side, correcting her, as he often told her it was his mission to help groom her for more important society.

He whispered loudly to Jane, "Men discuss business, Miss Hargreaves. Ladies, I believe, will adjourn through that door there to discuss... things of interest to women." He looked deep into Jane's eyes with a pleading expression, "Oh, do let the men have their cigars and brandy in peace."

2 CHAPTER 49: (APRIL 1776) Men Want Their Brandy and Ladies Want...

At the Wilson estate, just after the operatic performance, Jane was scolded by Mr. Tweedbottom. Mr. Tweedbottom, the tailor from Jane's Uncle Floyd's village, had taken it upon himself to educate Jane about... well, whatever he could, as he counted himself an authority on many topics.

Jane was indeed surprised when Mr. Tweedbottom arrived without having had sent word.

"That is a lovely coat you are wearing, Mr. Tweedbottom," Jane tried to change the subject as she commented on Mr. Tweedbottom's red velvet jacket.

Mr. Tweedbottom delighted in taking it upon himself to admonish the already well-bred Jane for asking the singer, Sir Henry Mossop, about what business the opera singer might be involved.

Jane did not suggest to Mr. Tweedbottom that she suspected Sir Henry Mossop was not a genuinely knighted "sir" at all.

Indeed, Jane held her tongue because Mr. Tweedbottom could very well be a suitor she should possibly have to consider, and she didn't want to be too particular. After all, Jane being single is why she and Silversmith came to the colonies in the first place.

"Miss Hargreaves," Mr. Tweedbottom shared, "I intend to start a fashion trend among men. Red velvet coats." He spoke with robust authority. He then added, "The women look eager to discuss matters of women in that room. You surely wish to join the ladies, don't you Miss Hargreaves?"

Jane had taken two steps away from the crowd, which was now splitting off.

Men were remaining to enjoy a sip of brandy and bit of snuff or smoke a pipe, while the ladies were slowly wending their way toward the door, presumably to cross the hallway into that other room.

Mr. Tweedbottom had indicated with a flourish that Jane should follow the laidies to do those things which are of interest to... well... women. Jane suspected he simply wanted an excuse to show her his lace cuffs flaring from under his red velvet sleeve to further impress her about his fashion sense.

Mr. Tweedbottom's outstretched arm passed but inches from her face and pointed to the door and the bustling skirts of the ladies exiting.

Jane had followed Mr. Tweedbottom's gaze and she turned to see Lady Sarah

Wilson was ushering all the ladies across the hall, leaving the men here in this drawing room where Mr. Mossop just had performed.

Jane politely forced a smile, bit her lip, and turned slowly to follow the other ladies.

The men had already begun to talk amongst themselves, satisfied that even if they were overheard, the women would be unable to comprehend the men's foreign language of business.

Being the last one through the door, Jane paused a moment and feigned to have forgotten something. Turning, she returned to a chair and reaching inside her long sleeve, extracted a handkerchief, which she balled up in her hand, so it would not reveal that she was actually placing that handkerchief on the chair.

Then, Jane picked up the cloth square by one corner so that it would flutter in the air as she feigned to have had retrieved it from the seat of the chair.

She wanted to make certain that if any of the men were watching her, it would indeed look as if she had forgotten something.

In reality, Jane simply wanted to hear what the men were discussing.

After all, because of the operatic performance by Sir Henry Mossop, there were several new faces which Jane did not recognize. She noticed her hostess, the dubious Lady Sarah Wilson, was shooing the women away from the men, as if Sarah Wilson were protecting her investment, yet still wanted to allow onlookers to admire her acquisitions of menfolk.

Sarah Wilson was now across the hall and instructing her slaves about some such matter or other.

As Jane slowly drifted toward the door to exit, she overheard one man with a large mustache speaking to another clean shaven fellow. "It's the only thing that makes economical sense. If they don't like the word 'slavery', they should just call it something else, but we will never make a profit unless we use free laborers."

Jane wished she could have been introduced to all the men, but she really was familiar only with the performer, Mr. Mossop, along with her tea drinking tailor-suitor Mr. Tweedbottom.

"I agree with you, Sir," Jane overheard Mr. Tweedbottom interject into the conversation.

The smooth shaven fellow added, "It is not as if we can create machines to harvest crops. Indeed, if the crown is willing to pay for our relationships with those natives to create an indentured class of rebels on this land, I say why not profit from it."

"Wasn't there to be another man, here? Our numbers seem off," a man with a beard commented. "Yes, but Mr. Hargreaves had a change of opinion," the man with the mustache had observed.

Slowly, Jane walked back toward the door so that she would not raise suspicions. Fortunately, the door across the hallway remained opened.

Yet another man with white powder in his hair and a red strip on his cuff, chimed in with, "How would the Crown ensure loyalty if it allowed its subjects to... to... form their own governance in another land... Nay, the Crown must enslave the rebel settlers. Teach them all a lesson!"

Jane was now back at the doorway across the hall. She had neglected to fully close the door behind her as she wanted to continue to hear what the men were saying for as long as possible.

Now one of the Wilson slaves came up and started to close the door. Before it had completely shut, Jane overheard Mr. Tweedbottom's voice saying, "Yes. She is the one whose Uncle was to come to Lady Sarah's, but... she came instead."

"Oh? Did he fall ill?" Another male

voice inquired.

Tweedbottom simply said, "I don't know why she came in his stead."

This response made Jane feel a knot in the pit of her stomach. Mr. Tweedbottom, after all, was there when her uncle Floyd had died... why did he simply dismiss it as if he didn't know?

Jane hesitated at the doorway of the room where the women were gathering. Some had brought needlepoint. Others had wanted to play cards. Still others were gossiping about something.

Jane was about to join the ladies when the booming voice of the opera singer abruptly penetrated the closed door of the room she had just left.

Sir Henry Mossop, the boisterous opera singer was loudly announcing, "Imagine, Floyd Hargreaves tried to convince me that employing white colonials as slaves... paying them fair wages no less... would somehow be more economical and provide a better product than simply using them as they were intended... as slaves who are grateful to work for room and board! Imagine!"

The other men laughed at such an absurd notion.

Although Jane could not see them, she reasoned they started to light their pipes as the waft of tobacco had billowed from underneath the door. She heard the clink of crystal cups, presumably filled with brandy or some other liquor, as they toasted, drank and smoked.

Then, one of Sarah Wilson's slaves noticed the room where the men were gathering was still open. The slave slowly walked over to close the door.

Jane realized both she and all the slaves in the Wilson house had arrived as colonists expecting opportunity. Instead, the Wilson slaves, pale, without hope, had lost their freedom. Somehow...

When Jane heard the lock click shut, she did not turn around to look. She could no longer hear the men and knew she would no longer be able to listen in to their conversations.

Jane felt a wave of frustration grip her. She stared into the open room where the ladies gathered. She stood betwixt the room of men and room of women.

Deciding. Seething. Contemplating.

She looked at the slave as he passed, but he averted his pale eyes. He did not speak, let alone offer to help or assist. He seemed so joyless, Jane thought.

"What," Jane asked herself very softly, "shall I do? Join the ladies for idle banter or get Silversmith and start packing?"

3 CHAPTER 50: (MAY 1776) Jane's Request to Visit Polly & John Dunlap's Conundrum

Jane sent Billy Dawes to present a message to Mrs. Dunlap, the printer's wife who was hosting Polly Mulhoolin, the woman they found on the side of the road. Jane wanted to visit with Polly, but was mindful of Mrs. Dunlap's schedule.

Billy Dawes returned to the estate of Sarah Wilson with information about the time Jane could visit. This was, after all, one of the reasons Jane had employed Billy Dawes for the season. Mr. Dawes had taken Jane in the carriage to the Dunlap residence several times already. Jane had met with both Mrs. Dunlap and Polly Mulhoolin to see how she was faring.

Outside in the small well-manicured garden of the Dunlap residence, both Jane and Polly lingered on two chairs under the shade of a tree. Simms, the butler, had set up a small table with two mugs and one pitcher of water filled with sliced lemon, strawberries, and diluted grape juice. The ladies refreshed themselves with sips of the beverage.

"Polly," Jane said, "I'm afraid that I suspect your husband might have been the victim of some men of business wishing to make a profit."

Polly took a sip, set down her mug and replied, "I must confess the same thought has occurred to me, as well, but I did not dare to utter it out loud."

"Well," Jane replied, "All I can say is I feel helpless in developing any plan to discover what has become of your husband. I don't know where to start."

Polly replied, "You have helped me tremendously, Jane. I just miss Button." "Would you want to return to your cabin to see if it still stands, Polly?" Jane asked.

Polly shook her head, "I'm in no condition to travel. Even if I could, I don't think I could bear it." She bit into a strawberry and then changed her tone when she asked Jane, "The season is nearly over. Will you be returning to your uncle's home?"

Jane replied hesitantly, "I do want to be a comfort and companion to you before the child arrives, but I have my own... concerns to attend to, you see... so I do not know."

"And...?" Polly asked. "And...what?" Jane asked in reply.

Polly shook her head, smiled, then said, "You mentioned you had questions about your Uncle's death. Did you find satisfactory answers? That is why you came out here in the first place, is it not? Did your friend, Mr. Tweedbottom help?"

"Oh, I suppose so..." Jane stated, shrugging her shoulders, "Somewhat. You see..." Jane's thought was interrupted by a loud commotion from within the Dunlap home. Both ladies hurried indoors as fast as they could.

Mr. John Dunlap was frustrated and red faced as he was engaged in an animated conversation with his wife. In his excitement, he had knocked over an urn filled with flowers decorating the table and one of the staff was already cleaning it up.

Mr. John Dunlap paid the servant no mind as he addressed his wife with strained tones, "I say we cannot print it in German because it will imply that German will be the main language on this land going forward."

"But," Mrs. Dunlap pleaded, "John, if you don't print it in German nor Dutch, most of the hard working settlers here who left the fatherland for a better life will feel rather slighted..."

Mr. Dunlap simply shook his head.

Mrs. Dunlap approached with a gentle touch and calmly suggested, "Why not wait to see if the English version gets signed? If it does, then you will know that it will be worth it to print up a German translation of it... Hmmm?"

Mr. John Dunlap sighed as he slumped into his chair. "Darling... Oh, my darling... That means that not only must I find somebody who can speak both English and German fluently, but somebody who has the diligence to translate the entire document, a document they may very well disagree with personally if they are loyal to their monarchy. I am not even addressing the fact that I would need to afford such a unicorn should I find him."

"Do not become overwhelmed, my little love," Mrs. Dunlap uttered in a diminutive tone neither Polly nor Jane had ever heard her use before.

"And penmanship," Mr. Dunlap

continued to protest, "This unicorn of many languages must also possess fine penmanship so I can discern when to set an F instead of an S for the press." John Dunlap sighed, exhausted by the thought of undertaking such a task.

"And you must find this person- your multi-lingual artistic unicorn- in secret," Mrs. Dunlap added with a playful smile.

"Thank you, my darling. I had forgotten to add discretion to the list of desirable traits..." He turned abruptly and shouted, "How am I to..." Mr. Dunlap stopped short as he saw the two ladies, Jane and Polly, standing in the doorway.

"Out of gratitude," Polly started, "for allowing me to remain here for my full term...I ...I would. Mr. Dunlap, I would be happy to share my language skills if you need something translated."

Mr. Dunlap looked at Polly from head to toe and sneered, "You?"

"Although," Polly started, "I arrived here in distress, back home I was educated and am fluent in German, as well as French and a bit of Italian and Latin. If it is discretion you require, I do not think, in my condition, I am at all fit to even leave your property."

Mr. Dunlap leaned forward, "But you do not know the importance of the document of which we speak."

"True. And if you do not feel I am a suitable candidate, then I shall respect that," Polly smiled.

"Oh, Mr. Dunlap, darling," Mrs. Dunlap started, "Polly must remain under my watch until the baby arrives, anyway."

Polly added, "In lieu of money, which I do not have, I would offer to compensate your gracious hospitality with translations, if you find that arrangement agreeable. And if you need to make your document public, I would be happy to keep my involvement a secret. No soul need know I translated it at all. I give you my word as a Mulhoolin from county Ulster."

"Then," Mr. John Dunlap took a step toward Polly, "before you offer your services, you must be aware of the nature of this document."

"Yes?" Polly asked a little uncertain and moved toward Jane for comfort.

"The colonies struggle," Mr. Dunlap started, "between other lands wishing to claim all thirteen as their own, against the desire to be self-governing. Still others interpret the concept of independence as worthy of a treasonous death, thinking we must have some sort of royalty to tax us, be it Spanish, Dutch, French, English or some other country."

He took a deep breath and added with a stern gaze, "The natives of this land do not understand the European methods of trade. Some Indians have been cheated, and feel resentful enough to justify revenge. Others, have been treated fairly and developed loyalties which blind them to other negotiations. Wars abound with every nation..." Then Mr. Dunlap spoke slowly, carefully saying each word, "This document could very well cause the rivers of conflict to flow with fresh and possibly innocent blood."

Mrs. Dunlap stepped forward toward the wide-eyed Polly Mulhoolin, "Now, do you still wish to translate? Until that adorable baby arrives, that is...hmmm?"

4 CHAPTER 51: (APRIL 1776) Carina Maria, the Messenger with Silversmith's Letter

Sunlight poured through the windows of the Hargreaves residence.

Witherspoon was in the kitchen, now sadly devoid of the cheery hellos with which his deceased employer, Floyd Hargreaves, used to greet him in the mornings. Witherspoon had still undertaken his duties, such as going into town on market day to procure food. However, he usually now purchased too much.

Witherspoon would select enough food to feed the temporary workers he would have to employ from time to time, but without Silversmith there, Witherspoon was the only fully employed staff at the Hargreaves residence.

Witherspoon enjoyed bringing home supplies for his employer Floyd Hargreaves, as well as the newly arrived niece, Jane, along with her lady's maid, Silversmith. To Witherspoon, that was a full household.

It was not, however, as grand as the large estate down the road. Witherspoon first met their staff in the market place, where one meets all the staff of the all the households in the village. The grand estate down the way employed a particular young lady toward which Witherspoon felt a particular affinity.

Carina Maria... She was one of the cooks. Her duties involved growing some foods in the garden, as well as shopping on market day.

Carina Maria... Witherspoon had been invited one day to visit her at her household where she had prepared for him a splendid onion soup which made him long to be in her company more frequently. She had told him then that she never got so many compliments on her cooking and felt Witherspoon was the most active supporter of her talents.

They had become professional friends. He had even asked her if Carina Maria could give a note to one of their carriage drivers so he could communicate with Silversmith as she tended to Miss Jane at the estate of Lady Sarah Wilson.

Carina Maria graciously agreed. How thoughtful. How else could Witherspoon get word to and from Silversmith to alert Mr. Tyler with updates.

Shaking off those thoughts, Witherspoon expected to receive Bryce Aiden Tyler shortly, as his visits were now more frequent since he took on the mission to prove his business partner, Floyd Hargreaves, had been murdered, and had not committed the shameful act of self-murder.

Witherspoon prepared a kettle with water and had just finished stoking the fires when his thoughts were interrupted by a knock at the front door.

He set the kettle down on the counter next to the tea cup reserved for Mr. Tyler, put on his jacket, assumed a rigid demeanor, and then strode to the door.

Without looking at the person standing at the other side of the door, Witherspoon simply opened it with a practiced, "Good morning, Sir."

But it was not Bryce Aiden Tyler. To his surprise, it was Carina Maria from the household at the grand estate.

"Good morning to you, Witherspoon," Carina Maria giggled, "But you needn't call me 'Sir'. Rather I prefer 'Carina Maria.'"

Carina Maria stood holding a folded note sealed with red wax. She wiggled it at Witherspoon. "Carina Maria!" Witherspoon exclaimed.

"Hello, again..." she smiled, "Our driver just returned and he gave me this. He collected it at the general store near Lady Sarah Wilson's property." She wiggled the folded paper in the air.

"Thank you! Can you come in?" Witherspoon asked opening the door wider.

"Oh, I wish I could, but his Lordship is expecting company and kitchen staff is going to be very busy. I was sent to the market for supplies and simply ran by here to give you this." She handed Witherspoon the letter and added in a whisper, "Is your employer's business partner, that Mr. Tyler, here? I know you said he's been coming by more frequently."

"Not yet, but I do expect him soon," Witherspoon replied holding the letter gingerly. "Mr. Tyler has had to work longer hours, trying to keep the business afloat. Mr. Hargreaves' death has been a hardship on everybody."

Carina Maria shared, "All our hearts go out to you and your household as you search for answers, Mr. Witherspoon. If you do not think your employer died by his own hand, then I pray you find the culprit who did... murder... him." She whispered the word, then added, "You are a trustworthy butler to remain here until his niece returns from her investigations. It must be difficult to adjust to an empty home."

"Thank you. Yes, Carina Maria, it has been difficult but Mr. Tyler's visits to conduct our experiments and investigations has been rewarding. We are all eager to find answers and then resume a normal routine."

Witherspoon smiled... something he seemed to only do when Carina Maria was present. "Your visits. These messages..." Witherspoon's voice cracked, "...have provided me a comfort I cannot quite articulate, Carina Maria."

"Oh, Mr. Witherspoon, you are a very gracious butler, indeed... I am only happy to act as messenger just to see you smile when you get a letter from Silversmith. That is reward enough for me. Mr. Hargreaves was a good man. Mr. Tyler is also a good man,"

Carina Maria reached out and touched Witherspoon's hand holding the letter as she continued, "My heart breaks to see wholesome people struck by such a tragedy, Mr. Witherspoon." She smiled with sad eyes.

"You are always compassionate... I feel fortunate knowing your household is... is... nearby..." Witherspoon managed to reply in a hoarse whisper.

Brightly, Carina Maria changed the subject with a cheery smile, "Well, I best be getting back. I wouldn't want cook to fret about me being delayed and all... I expect your Mr. Tyler will be here soon and I cannot have him think you've been neglecting your duties."

She playfully shook a finger at him, then touched his arm, and pointed to his name written on the front of the document she was still holding. "Show Mr. Tyler this letter. Perhaps it will provide another clue so you can solve this perplexing puzzle. Then, when Mr. Tyler leaves, you are invited to come by after we serve the family afternoon tea. If I am out in the vegetable garden, one of the kitchen maids can fetch me and we can talk about... about whatever you'd like to..."

Witherspoon replied, "I am afraid my conversation would be tedious as I am trying to discover what project Mr. Hargreaves worked on without Mr. Tyler's knowledge which would generate a motive in somebody to commit murder. I cannot find anything tangible, yet I feel there must be something... or perhaps it is my pride to escape the shadow of my master having committed self-murder..."

She said, "You will find the evidence you need. Be patient."

"..And then, I awaken at night," Witherspoon hurriedly added, "wondering if the allowance Silversmith told me Miss Jane gets would be sufficient to support this entire household... including me..."

"I can always ask our butler," Carina Maria added, "...if there might be a position for you with us..." She smiled, curtsied, and added, "I must be going, Witherspoon. I hope to see you later today." She hurried off and called over her shoulder, "After tea is served to his Lordship..."

Witherspoon watched her retreat, and smiled. He lingered at the door, not wanting to close it until she disappeared over the horizon.

Carina Maria always brought a smile and a laugh with her. That is why he looked forward to market day... for the chance to see her there... He wondered if she would ever consider him as a romantic prospect. Surely not, if she had to get him employment in her own household. No. He had to find another way to show that he was a true butler, able to run a household no matter what life presented.

Yet, Carina Maria worked in a grand estate where both the owners were born into their titles, whereas Witherspoon had worked for a man of the middling trades.

Yet, she never reminded Witherspoon of this fact. Witherspoon knew, even if he did ask the butler of the grand estate for a position, he would be lucky to get the title of under butler... but they already had one. Perhaps he could be an experienced footman.

He found it so astounding that a woman such as Carina Maria, a member of kitchen staff devoted to his Lordship, would invite him to be her friend. How was it that when he confessed his fears to her, he still felt like a strong man encouraged to take the next bold step?

Yet, Witherspoon knew he had to settle affairs in his own life before he could present Carina Maria with the possibility of considering him for something greater than friendship. No, he could not work in the same household as Carina Maria unless they were...

Witherspoon suddenly noticed the clock and quickly closed the heavy wooden door behind him. He rushed to the kitchen and set the kettle upon the fire. Then, he paused for one moment as he recalled the fresh memory of Carina Maria's hand touching his.

He smiled and shook himself back to his stoic butler persona. Then, he noticed he was still holding the unopened letter Carina Maria had just given to him. Mr. Bryce Aiden Tyler would be here any moment to continue in their unofficial investigation into the death of Floyd Hargreaves, uncle to Jane Hargreaves.

Again, he looked at the unopened letter in his hand, took a deep breath, then went to the writing desk in the foyer, placing the unopened letter on top so he could share the news with Mr. Tyler when he arrived.

Witherspoon hurried back into the kitchen and then heard a rapid knock at the front door.

5 CHAPTER 52: (APRIL 1776) Bryce, Witherspoon, Letters, Latches and Chalk

The afternoon sun beamed through a window of the Hargreaves residence in town. Witherspoon had just put the kettle on the fires in the kitchen when he heard a knock at the front door.

Bryce Aiden Tyler stood there as Witherspoon opened the door and started to greet Mr. Tyler in the usual fashion when Mr. Tyler simply walked in past him.

It was time for them to continue investigating the circumstances surrounding the death of Floyd Hargreaves, Jane's uncle.

The Butler, Witherspoon, closed the door behind Mr. Tyler, walked to his writing desk in the foyer, and announced to Bryce Aiden Tyler, "Sir, a letter has arrived. I assume from Silversmith." He indicated the folded paper to Mr. Tyler, pointing to the address. Witherspoon said, "It is addressed, you see, to myself, Mr. Witherspoon. Hopefully answers and news lay within."

Bryce strode to Witherspoon, took the letter out of the butler's hand, broke the wax seal, and read it right there near the foyer writing desk Witherspoon himself often used to note events of the household for his records.

"Oh! . This was addressed to you, not me. My apologies, Witherspoon," Bryce stated while still reading the letter. "My thirst for new information must have over ridden my manners," he commented while still reading.

Bryce continued with, "It appears that Miss Jane will be remaining at that Sarah Wilson home. Jane says she suspects her uncle was going to buy a slave for the purposes of converting him to a servant on salary, or freeing him. This act would have angered some men of business, she suspects. Cutting into their profits, she says, by letting other slaves think the same options apply to them." Bryce looked up in disbelief, "She intends to remain a while longer to investigate with Silversmith," Bryce stated, frustrated.

"So, it appears Miss Jane and Silversmith won't return as we originally thought?"

"No... No..." Bryce seemed troubled and distracted as he continued, "Something that Mr. Tweedbottom said bothers me. Those men who came in and then left when they saw us... The ones with the red design on their cuffs, that fashion hallmark Mr. Tweedbottom is urging all men to adopt. I am uncertain how to state this, Witherspoon. If I review all the facts together, this seems innocuous, yet there is something which I cannot discern."

"An uneasy feeling, Mr. Tyler?" Witherspoon clarified.

"Yes, Witherspoon," Bryce Aiden Tyler confirmed. "Recent events should be clear, yet feels obscured and I am unable to articulate why." He sat in the chair of the writing desk.

"Sir?" Witherspoon asked.

"The tailor's chalk. Where is it?" Bryce Aiden Tyler suddenly changed subjects and stood up.

"I believe we placed it on a table in the kitchen, Sir, with the other items procured from the General Store." The Butler asked, "Shall I fetch it?".

"Do," Bryce Aiden smiled. "Then off to the study where the deed was done," Bryce stated as he stomped toward the study.

Once inside, Bryce walked on the floor gingerly.

He watched as his own footprint was created in the dust. He placed his foot on the undisturbed dust, carefully picked up his foot, and noticed the print he left.

Then, he replaced his foot into the same print and picked it up to determine if he could step there twice while giving the impression of having only stepped there once.

Bryce Aiden Tyler was curious as to why there would not be any foot prints at all when clearly, even if Floyd Hargreaves had killed himself, he would have had to have walked to the desk himself. Yet there were no foot prints of any sort... only prints of the doctor, the magistrate, and the magistrate's brother as they walked in to examine and then remove the body.

While waiting for Witherspoon to come to the study with the chalk, Bryce Aiden Tyler walked halfway across the room, then stopped to look behind him at his trail of footprints.

He looked at the window straight ahead and the undisturbed dust before him. He took a few steps backwards to see if he could step back into the prints he had just made without disturbing the original prints.

At the doorway, Witherspoon appeared, waiting, and holding the tailor's chalk. He cleared his throat to alert the back-ward walking Mr. Tyler that Witherspoon had arrived.

Bryce froze, midway and tried to twist around without moving his feet. He briefly made eye contact with Witherspoon, yet was unable to maintain the twist and simply said, "Oh, good fellow. You found the tailor chalk. Excellent. Now, may I ask you, Witherspoon, if your kitchen has one of those devices invented by François Boullie? I forget what they are called."

Witherspoon thought a moment and

then recollected, "Ah. I believe you mean the cheese shredder, Sir. I shall return immediately." Witherspoon placed the tailor chalk at the entrance to the study and left to retrieve the cheese shredder from the kitchen.

Bryce remained staring at his own feet, deep in thought. Bryce called after the butler, "And cheese cloth, Witherspoon, if you would."

The always fastidiously dressed butler returned with the cheese grater and folded cheese cloth.

"Sir, I see you have not collected the chalk. Would you like me to hand it to you along with the cheese grater and cheese cloth?"

"Allow me to make my way to you," Bryce continued as he walked backwards stepping into his own footprints until he reached the hallway and then moved to the hall to collect the items Witherspoon held.

Bryce Aiden Tyler strode to the writing table in the hallway and laid out the cheese cloth. Then he situated the cheese grater and started to grate the tailor's chalk into a powder, piling it up in the center of the cheese cloth.

Witherspoon was mildly concerned about the state of his writing table, which he always kept pristine, but made no mention of the faint powdery outline left behind as Bryce Aiden Tyler collected the corners of the cheese cloth and laid the cheese grater on the desk.

Bryce smiled proudly. "I never thought something invented in the 1540's would come in handy during our modern age of the 1770's"

He hurried back into the study, but this time the cloth was filled with chalk dust. Witherspoon followed silently and waited at the entrance of the study as Bryce found his original footprints and once again attempted to step in the set he had just made. This time, as he took a step, he twisted behind him and tapped the cloth to release a fine powder of chalk, which did indeed cover the prints he had just made on the wooden floor.

"Do you see?" Bryce asked Witherspoon, "I am hiding the footprints I just made."

He would take a step, then tap the cheesecloth to release a cloud of chalk dust. Take another step, then release more dust. Light clouds of dust slowly drifted to the floor covering the footprint, but also clinging to the fibers on his trousers and the tops of his shoes. Witherspoon, fastidious valet, had to avert his eyes to avoid making a comment.

"Very clean, eh? I've just mastered how a ghost would move across the room. What think you, Witherspoon?" Bryce asked with hands on his hips admiring his work as he now stood in the middle of the room with no visible footprints. It did indeed look as if he had just appeared in the center of the room.

Witherspoon was resistant to comment at first, but then blurted out, "Chalk dust... on your shoes and the legs of your trousers."

He looked away. Had he said too much? Been too bold? Would Mr. Tyler react with anger over this observation?

It is just that part of Witherspoon's duties was to be a valet and ensure his employer was dressed appropriately and to date, chalk dust was not an appropriate accessory for any occasion. He bit his lip to avoid saying anything more.

"Oh, right..." Bryce added as he looked at his legs with the dust marks, "that means that if the killer did this... Witherspoon, did you notice anybody that day with excessive dust on their shoes or skirts or the legs of their trousers?"

"I did not, sir," Witherspoon replied.

"Then, perhaps they had to change

clothes," Bryce thought aloud, then added, "Witherspoon, this study... Are there any secret passages of any sort I am not aware of, which would allow ingress or egress to this house?"

"No, Mr. Tyler," the Butler explained as he remained at the doorway. "The only entrances to this room are this doorway, which I am now occupying, and... the window over there."

6 CHAPTER 53: (MARCH 1776) Button, Wake Up.

In the midst of seemingly endless horizons, the Farmer peered at a statuesque, tall, raven haired Indian who seemed to appear from nowhere.

Then, the farmer looked at his oxen, grazing; his cart, filled with jugs of water; the sun, very close to setting; and then the limp figure of Button, still unconscious.

Without a word, the farmer shook his head. He walked casually to his cart and grabbed a jug of fresh sweet water. He strode toward a large tree, crouched at the base of the trunk and pulled aside a large mossy branch to reveal a small entrance.

The Indian fellow, stepped over the unconscious Button, untangled his leg from the leather reins of the farmer's cart, effortlessly picked him up, and carried Button through the tiny doorway in the trunk of the tree.

The moss covered branch over the trunk of the hallowed out tree concealed the opening of the cavern, which was large enough for the men to stand upright. Some of the rocks of the cave allowed for light beams of sunset to stream through. The dead hallow tree trunk acted as a chimney and there was already a small fire burning, smoke billowing up and out of the top of the trunk, like a natural chimney.

Inside, the Indian fellow glanced at a pile of folded woven blankets. The farmer understood, took one, and set it out on the ground. The Indian fellow then placed Button onto the blanket.

The farmer knelt beside Button, then took his jug of water and splashed Button's face.

Button awoke with a start, coughing and blinking the water away from his eyes. Distraught, he continued his vehement diatribe as if there were no interruption, "You sir," Button spat at the Farmer, "are a devious trickster. "

"Foolish to assume all men have ill intent," the farmer drawled.

"Only a trickster would try to convince a fool to not act like a fool to play into his web of foolery!" Button retorted as he looked down, "Ha! Do you plan to sleep on either side of me, trapping me as the others did?"

Button scrambled to his feet.

"You are free to run out into the dark where both criminal and wild beast hunt," the farmer shouted, then added, "But here there is food, shelter, water. In the morn, I will go to town..." The farmer paused, "If you wish, you may join me."

"You expect me," Button turned, "to... to believe... to..." Button's hand rubbed his forehead as he tried to make sense of all which had recently befallen him. Then, Button added, "to remain with you, a farmer who won't speak... and a savage who can't speak?"

"But, I do speak English," the tall Indian fellow said with soothing tones. "What?" Button spun around to face the Indian, "What? What?"

"To assume," the statuesque fellow started, "all Indians you meet operate like Indians you have recently met, is akin to assuming all men are equally good or equally bad." He smiled, "One must take time to learn the character of each individual."

Button choked on his words as he stuttered. He stood, fists clenched. "Are... you... attempting trickery of voice, as Pythia, the Ancient Greek Delphi Oracle priestess of Apollo? The gastromyth?" Button's face turned red, "The arts of ventriloquy," he accused.

The farmer gaped at Button, "Eh? I'm a farmer." And then he looked at the tall native man helplessly, adding, "I can't speak like that."

"You enact ventriloquism and put eloquent words into that man's mouth," Button reiterated to the Farmer.

"Don't be mad," the farmer urged. "TallMan here can help you. He will not scalp you. Your fears are misplaced. You are not being held prisoner in any way."

The towering Indian fellow walked to a basket of food and pointed to some fire kindling, "This tree is hallow and the trunk conceals a stone cave in the knoll. That acts as a chimney, so I use that corner to cook food. I am a medicine man who has completed travelling. I sought to learn medicine from any man of foreign language who would share knowledge with me. I am slowly wending my way north, back to my home."

"Your home? This is not your home? Where are the others? In the other trees?" Button asked.

"My tribe," TallMan explained, "My family, is north. In Canada. In my pursuit of the knowledge of healing, I learned something else."

"What was that?" Button asked, curious instead of afraid, as he sat back down on the blanket. TallMan now took food from the basket and placed it on several smooth rocks, warming in the fire.

TallMan replied to Button with, "Men of any land can have a greedy heart. Greed breeds trickery. Tribes have been falsely accused of kidnapping Colonists, for destroying the property of Colonists. Some are guilty. Some are hired to do it. Some are blamed because they have my skin-color."

"And?" Button prodded.

"And," TallMan answered, "It is an

injustice to use innocent tribes to incur fear in the hearts of the Colonists. It   is how do you Europeans say... theatrics. Especially when it is Colonists who hire renegade tribesmen to carry out the kidnappings."

"Do you know who was behind... who ordered the attack on me?" Button blurted out.

"No," TallMan replied, "But if you were attacked by Indian fellows and not harmed, it is likely they were hired to sell you as a slave. It is likely the man who hired those fellows was a Colonist himself... if you were truly attacked. Your story is actually common in these parts. You are lucky Farmer found you."

The Farmer took a stick and flipped the fish over on the hot rock so the other side would cook. Some vegetables were also roasting. Another basket held freshly gathered herbs which the farmer ripped up and spread over the top of the fish, adding to the intoxicating aroma.

Button was famished. The farmer passed a jug of water to Button, urging him to drink. It crossed Button's mind to remain until these men slept and then to escape and run away... again... but he was not sure it was his best move. He was exhausted, after all. He wouldn't know in which direction to run. He deliberated as he inhaled the smoky aroma of food.

TallMan unfolded another blanket and laid it out for himself far away from Button and far away from the entrance to let Button know he was free to go at any time. Likewise, the Farmer took a blanket for himself and set it by the stony wall far from Button, given the confined space of the cave.

Button asked, "TallMan, that is your name, is it not?"

"It is," TallMan replied.

"Farmer appears to be familiar with... well, everything. How frequently has he been here?" Button asked.

"He stops on his way to deliver water to town," TallMan shared. "He calls it Meeting Town, but I'm sure it has some official name."

"But, most towns have their own source of water. A well, perhaps?" Button countered, "Why bring water from so far away?"

Farmer explained, "They need to trust that the water is pure. I guarantee it. The meetings take a long time." The farmer reached into a leather pouch inside his jacket and poured out a pinch of salt into the palm of his hand. He sprinkled it onto the meat, fish and vegetables on the hot rocks.

The farmer asked Button, "Have you heard the word 'Apache'?"

"There are numerous tribes around. I think that may be one of them?" Button guessed.

"Apache is Zuni for 'enemy'," the farmer explained to Button. "Apaches are thirsty for a fight."

"To fight other tribes, or the colonists?" Button asked.

TallMan spoke, "Legend says that around your year 1300, the local tribes suffered drought in the land, making food scarce. One traveler spoke of meeting a stranger from a land of ice up north. This ice-stranger had a curved stick with springy sinews and a shorter straight branch, stripped of leaves and with a sharp point at the end."

"That sounds like a bow and arrow," Button commented.

TallMan continued, "This new weapon allowed the strangers to win wars from a distance and help win territories with sources of water from tribes without such sophisticated weaponry. Thus started an ongoing conflict between farming tribes and hunting tribes."

The Farmer added in a whisper, "If a man needs to prove his bravery by killing with a new weapon, that gives him unfair advantage... He is hiding behind the tool and is not brave at all."

Button lowered his voice to the farmer, saying, "I am glad to see you are becoming more loquacious." Then to TallMan, Button said, "And of what importance is this history lesson to me?"

"My people," TallMan explained, "have endured the same attacks you have just undergone. I could have been a warrior, but chose to explore and learn about healing."

"I don't think you could comprehend," Button started, "the greed of the British Crown, and how it may drive people to unmentionable actions."

"Greed?" TallMan repeated.

TallMan took a drink of water from the jug and said, "Have you heard of a Spaniard named Francisco Vasquez Coronado, who was searching for the seven cities of Cibola."

"Around two hundred years ago," the farmer said.

TallMan added, "To be precise, 1540."

"No," Button bluntly stated.

"Coronado's greed," TallMan explained, "drove him to hunt for gold in the legendary El Dorado. However, the lands of the Zuni had no gold. No tribe welcomed him, but he hunted for this gold with unreasonable passion. Like Coronado, greed has propelled explorers to look for a fabled treasure, which never existed. This has been going on for centuries. That greed has wounded the lands, introduced new diseases, and killed our people. We did not invite these invasions. Like an undisciplined child, they angrily destroyed the places where they felt entitled to find a treasure, but where there was none."

"A tantrum resulted in the slayings of innocent tribes,"the Farmer added, "and slavery..."

"I am sorry to hear that, Mr. TallMan," Button interjected now more sympathetic.

But the Farmer corrected Button. "TallMan's people do not have surnames."

"Pardon me?" Button replied, confused.

Farmer explained, "Their names describe."

TallMan clarified, "We have two names, one used in private and one to describe ourselves, a name we can use when trading. My name is TallMan, not Mister TallMan. I am tall. I am a man. This name describes me."

"But, I thought your names would be more... colorful..." Button added.

"Since the pilgrims arrived," said TallMan, "all tribes had to create a public name just to conduct business and trade with the settlers. You have a Christian name, which your family uses, and a surname, which the public uses. Your full name is the first name and the last name. Likewise in my tribe, we have a public name we use for the European accounting, so that we can get paid if hired by them," TallMan clarified.

"You mean a name like Running Bear? Soaring Eagle?"

"No," the farmer explained. "The British give those names to be poetic."

TallMan gave an example, "My mother was raised in the brave Bear clan. My father was of the Wolf clan. Both clans assumed boys would be active in honor, in hunting, in providing, in protecting. As a child, I did not want to work and was timid. My father called me FrozenFoot, because I was stuck or frozen in place. My mother always told me she would pray I would become brave like the Bears. She was adopted by the Bear family when she was a girl. That was my goal, to outgrow FrozenFoot and become a brave bear. When I did mature, I picked my name of TallMan."

Button asked, "So when did you... become brave like a bear?"

"When I was an older boy," TallMan started, "I learned my tribe had an alliance with a group of LongCoats, who taught us English. They also taught us the ways of *Doodaa-Tsaahi*. My mother took on another name, a third name, to honor Doodaa-Tsaahi. I became bold, and set out to explore and learn the healing ways of different peoples to take the best healing practices back to my people."

"Doodaa-Tsaahi," the farmer explained, "is Navajo for Christian Messiah."

"Messiah?" Button asked.

"TallMan's mother became Catholic," the farmer added.

"Catholic? But my wife is Catholic," Button explained. "Well, her father was Catholic and that was enough to force her to leave Ireland and become a servant here in the colonies... The

English view the Irish as a pool of cheap labor."

"Perhaps we are more alike than different," TallMan smiled.

"But the Navajo are a bloodthirsty warring tribe," Button announced. "Are you Navajo?"

"Navajo means Great Planted Fields," Tall man shared. "The Navajo are great farmers. Doodaa-Tsaahi had charged the tribe with protecting the lands. In return, the soil produces crops of food and medicine." He then thoughtfully paused, "I have given you hints about my mother and which tribe raised her. But, now I do not think it wise to give you any more information about me, lest you judge me on your perception of that group. A group, or tribe, I only know as family. You should invest the time to know me 'TallMan', not me 'the Indian from that tribe'. Understand why I make the choices I do. Then, judge me as you wish."

The farmer interjected, "Didn't TallMan just say to get to know each man's character by getting to know him?"

TallMan concurred, "I did. I think I will speak of the tribes I have met, healed, warred with or befriended. I do not think I will speak any more about a tribe to which I may or may not belong."

"Why?" Button asked.

TallMan replied, "If I take the time to learn the arts of healing from many places... If I take the time to learn your English language. Then I must ask that you take the time to learn about me without assuming I will act as those you have met, just because we may share similar physical traits."

There was a silence.

Farmer was the one who broke in, this time, "As a farmer, I grow food. I wonder if I could grow medicine as a crop."

"I would think that if you grew some

medicine," Button commented, "that some greedy soul would try to own it. Only permitting others to get at it in exchange for power and money, disregarding any treaty as long as it might lead to profit."

TallMan replied, "There will always be people with deceitful hearts. A man of any race can wound the earth which gives us food, sacrifice lives, then dismiss his part in the crime, shirk responsibility and say, 'time will heal any who feel offended. I do not need to do anything to fix what I have done.' Time will not heal criminal acts unless retribution is sought."

The farmer added, "Some will think they will never suffer consequences."

TallMan observed, "I cannot heal the disease of power and greed fueled by insatiable lust."

"Lust?" Button asked

"For a shiny button off a soldier's

uniform," TallMan explained, "some will agree to kidnap, scalp, or murder. Greed infects all people. But not all people wish to be free of that disease. When you find those who feel no shame, you must contain them so they do not infect others. If you cannot, then you must avoid them."

Button nodded, "The popular teaching today is to be dissatisfied with what you have and yearn for an easier faster way to riches... even if it means turning a blind eye to what is right and wrong."

The farmer asked, "Have you heard of the Mohawks?"

"The Mohawks! They say they love to scalp!" Button became alarmed.

TallMan explained, "They are the tribe of Abenaki." TallMan continued, "I have healed and made friends in several tribes throughout the lands. My mother came from the Mohawks. " he smiled.

7 CHAPTER 54: (APRIL 1776) Bryce and Witherspoon Investigate a Child's Game

Bryce took a deep breath and said to Witherspoon, "Let us continue our analysis of how this deed transpired. We must prove Mr. Hargreaves did not commit self-murder if we are to ask the Magistrate for assistance."

"We have already established that the possible murderer could have hidden his footprints by using chalk dust and we also know there are only two ways to gain entrance to this room," Witherspoon reiterated.

"And it is not likely the killer would have used the locked door which none of us could open until I removed the pins in the door hinges." Bryce added, "Which means, entrance and exit must have been through that window."

Bryce hesitated as his thoughts raced and snarled against each other like tangled horse reins. He took a deep breath as he became aware of his heart pounding.

"Is it possible, Witherspoon? Is it possible." Bryce said aloud.

"What, sir? Is what possible?" Witherspoon asked.

"You did not notice anybody visiting the house that day with chalk on their clothing. Is that what you said? And you would have noticed, correct?" Bryce asked.

"I did not see any chalk and I would have noticed, Sir," Witherspoon replied.

"So," Bryce thought out loud, "Then perhaps the deed was committed earlier in the day to give the murderer time to clean off his clothing or change his clothes."

"But, sir," Witherspoon commented, "You are assuming the murderer did not kill Mr. Hargreaves and then just leave. Why are you implying that he or she was in this household, killed Mr. Hargreaves, and then returned to this house?"

"Because," Bryce explained, "because the gossipy townsfolk you talked with cannot agree to the same time they heard the shot. That means there were at least two shots and one must have been a decoy. If there was a decoy, then our murderer wanted to be seen in a public setting when the false shot went off to make him or her appear innocent. If we are dealing with two shots and disappearing footprints, then you, Witherspoon, may have encountered the murderer the day Floyd Hargreaves was killed."

"I see, Sir. Hmmm..." Witherspoon uttered.

"Therefore," Bryce continued, "I must ask you this, Witherspoon. Is it possible your employer, Mr. Hargreaves, was killed earlier in the day and left alone in the study? Were you, Witherspoon, distracted by any task which deviated from your regular daily routine and did this task prevent you from checking in on Mr. Hargreaves? As you normally would have done?"

"Are you asking me at what time of day did I last tend to Mr. Hargreaves's requests, Mr. Tyler?" Witherspoon clarified.

"Indeed I am." Bryce confirmed.

"There was a project Silversmith asked me to help her with," Witherspoon replied.

"Ah, and what was this project?" Bryce asked.

"It was of a personal nature for Miss Jane, Sir. I am not at liberty to discuss it." the butler replied.

"Indeed, Witherspoon. Well, can you share if it took you away from your other duties? Did it consume your day?" Bryce asked.

"It took the better part of two days. I did set everything else aside. Mr. Hargreaves had given me permission to tend to Miss Jane, as he wanted her to feel comfortable here during her time of transition to the Colony," Witherspoon explained.

"And you also had to get supplies for the tea Jane was to have with Mr. Tweedbottom?" Bryce prodded.

"Yes, sir. That took me out of the house while Silversmith was upstairs sewing," Witherspoon replied, "I only emerged from my back room when Mr. Tweedbottom arrived at the front door. In fact," Witherspoon stopped.

"Yes?" Bryce prodded.

"Well, a minor point. Not worth mentioning, Sir," Witherspoon replied.

"Everything is worth mentioning. Permit me the opportunity to dismiss it after I have heard it. Please," Bryce Aiden Tyler urged.

"Although I cannot discuss the nature of the project for Miss Jane, I can say that Silversmith told me the reason Miss Jane asked for our assistance, Silversmith and myself, was because it had to do with a comment made by Mr. Tweedbottom."

"Oh, I think that bit of information is rather noteworthy, Witherspoon. I am glad you shared that," Bryce started. "Let me review the facts: I do not think that Silversmith has any motive to kill Mr. Hargreaves, nor does Jane. So that means that if you and Silversmith were doing the jobs of ten servants... If you were both intent upon conducting your tasks with discretion and competence, as

I know you are wont to do, then is it possible?" He shook his head.

"Is what possible, Mr. Tyler?" Witherspoon asked.

"That Mr. Tweedbottom, a man with obvious affection for Jane, would wish to create the illusion that he were in two places at once? But what would be his motive? Or is there somebody else who felt it necessary to usher Mr. Hargreaves to heaven? Whoever it was must have come here earlier in the day, knowing you and Silversmith would be occupied, killed Mr. Hargreaves, and then later appeared again with a false shot sound to appear innocent of the act of murder. This took a bit of planning."

"Very good, Sir," Witherspoon commented.

"Witherspoon, could you fetch that children's fishing game?" Bryce walked to the window and started to examine it.

"Very well, Sir," Witherspoon removed

himself and headed to the kitchen to retrieve the toy. Witherspoon then appeared at the window outside, surprising Bryce by tapping on the window pane.

"An interesting choice, Witherspoon," Bryce started as he opened the window, "To come outside and to the window..."

"If, as you said, Sir, the murderer came and went through this window, then I felt perhaps I would be of more use to examine it from the outside as you are from the inside, Sir," Witherspoon suggested.

"Who would have wanted to kill Floyd Hargreaves, Witherspoon?" Bryce asked aloud.

"I have given this matter some thought, Sir," Witherspoon replied.

"And?" Bryce prodded.

"He had several business associates who disagreed with him, but nothing which would offend their honor, require a dual, nor demand blood to atone for the offense. I have spoken with the staff of the other households with which Mr. Hargreaves conducted business so feel I have an accurate depiction of the general attitude toward Mr. Hargreaves."

"I see..." Bryce continued while examining the frame of the window, opening it a bit.

"But I also had to evaluate if you, Sir, had motive to kill your business partner," Witherspoon stated.

"I?" Bryce Aiden Tyler stopped and looked at Witherspoon, perplexed.

"Yes, sir, but I am assisting you in this matter because I have evaluated that after Mr. Hargreaves' death, your amount of work increased. You are now burdened with debts due to accounts not being paid in time as Mr. Hargreaves was the one to do that. You have no financial nor other gain by his death. In fact, it is a burden for you to even take time to investigate, yet I know you are unable to sleep with unanswered questions, so this investigation you asked me to help with is a sincere attempt to find out what really happened. Ergo, you did not do this foul deed."

"Well thought through, Witherspoon. Accurate, my good fellow. I do want to find out the truth. Thank you for considering the notion and dismissing me as your suspect," Bryce smiled.

"Likewise," Witherspoon continued, "I do not have motive because with my employer dead, I have no source of income. Miss Jane has a fixed income, so when she does return, if she decided to keep me on, then my salary would remain fixed. Neither Jane, nor Silversmith, nor I have any motive. We all wanted things to continue on as they had been, but..." Witherspoon shrugged, then added, "So I have eliminated you, sir, Miss Jane, and Silversmith as people who would have wanted to kill Floyd Hargreaves, may he rest in peace." He sighed.

"Then let us continue the investigation, Witherspoon. Let us come up with something to change Magistrate Pinkney's mind. Please hand me the child's toy," Bryce asked as he opened the window a bit more.

"Well," Witherspoon started as he handed the fishing pole and paper fish through the window.

"Well, what?" Bryce put his hand on his hip.

"It's just that from out here, from this angle," Witherspoon started, "I can see a trail of fresh white powder, which is a bit brighter than dust... so... one would have to have taken the chalk over the majority of this room to remove all traces of footprints after placing Mr. Hargreaves' body at that big desk over there. They would have been in this room for some time, while Silversmith and I were in the same house..."

"Now is not the time for regrets and guilt, Witherspoon. Concentrate on the task at hand," Bryce started. "Here I will close the window, but take the pole and the magnet at the end of the pole and see if you can close the latch from the outside using the power of the magnet."

Witherspoon nodded. He took the pole and waited for Bryce to close the window, but left the latch undone. From the outside, Witherspoon attempted to use the magnet and draw the metal latch down to close.

It did not work at first, but then the butler hit the window with light repeated taps, and the latch swung down. Witherspoon then used the magnet to maneuver the latch into a locked position. And the window locked from the outside.

Excited, Mr. Tyler unlocked the window and reached out to shake Witherspoon's hand.

"Well done, Witherspoon. We just figured out how the ghost left this room in a very human form."

"And now, Sir?" the Butler started, "We only need to learn how our ghost was able to create a shot, which sounded as if it came from this room, without being in the room, without shooting through the window, and without breaking any glass."

"Ah, yes..." Bryce looked around the room, then back at Witherspoon, "Well, you had best come back inside then, Witherspoon. Our small victory has not yet led to a complete solution." Bryce looked at his feet again as if they might tell him something.

8 CHAPTER 55: (MARCH 1776) Button Decides to Stay

Button decided not to run away from the protection of TallMan's tree-trunk hide-away cave. He looked up at the opening in the roof where smoke from the fire was escaping, and saw it was nighttime. He reasoned if these two men intended harm, they would have restrained him, by now.

Button was tempted to run away after they slept, but he listened as the Farmer had said, "If you run, you'll never find your wife..."

Button took a deep breath. Realized

finding his wife was a very slim chance, indeed. In her condition, she was probably already devoured by a wild animal. But, if there was a chance, a very small chance, he was honor-bound to take it.

"The Navajo understand the land," TallMan shared. "My mother's forgiveness showed kindness to those around her, to those who did not deserve it. She even taught Farmer how to increase crops in this land."

Button looked at Farmer.

Farmer replied, "In Europe, corn is grown to feed the livestock. But, we learned we cannot serve corn to our chickens because they won't lay eggs... or the ones that do, the chicks die when they hatch."

"Indeed," Button had commented. "I have been wondering what to do with my acres and thought of growing corn. Our chickens in the rear of our cabin eat vegetable scraps from our table and some grains," Button shared, feeling more comfortable, now.

"My family grew corn in our first year," the Farmer continued, "but we found ears were not forming. Then, we learned from TallMan's mother that we needed to bury a whole fish along the row as we planted seed. When the ears started to form and the silks started to show, we boiled the fat of an animal, skimmed it off while it was still warm liquid, and poured it on the tips of the ears... on the silks... to seal out the bugs and to keep the kernels sweet and juicy."

Button replied, "I was thinking of growing corn to feed to my chickens, but I did not know it would weaken them."

"Corn is only to be fed to four legged hoofed creatures," Farmer replied. "Do you see how Europeans can learn from the tribes?"

"LongCoats understand the ways of the lands they come from," TallMan started. "I have learned medicine from them, but

LongCoats did not understand that one must respect the earth before she can bear fruits for man to eat."

"Who is this LongCoat, he refers to?" Button whispered to Farmer.

"In winter, the Dutch wore coats, which dragged on the ground, " the Farmer replied.

TallMan added, "Most native tribesmen would never wear such clothing, which encumbered their movements. The Europeans, those from the Netherlands, the Dutch... wear the long coats, so we call them the LongCoats."

"But, tribesmen refer to us as 'pale-face?" Button asked genuinely perplexed.

Farmer clarified, "The Irish are pale. French, Spaniards, Southern Italy are dark. What we all have in common is our strange fabric clothing... the length of our coats in winter."

"How many tribes are there in these lands where kings have started colonies?" Button asked.

TallMan looked up and then spoke, "Of the native tribes I have met and made friends with, I count the Adirondacks, Cherokees, Creeks, Delawares, Zuni, Wyandots, Six Nations, Shawnees, Senecas."

"Remember the Raritans, Otaris, and Pequaots," Farmer added.

"Yes..." TallMan smiled. "I have also met the Sandusky, Narragansetts, Mission and Mandan tribes, but I have also met many Europeans and others during my years of travel."

TallMan, feeling thirsty, reached for fresh water. He filled up his mouth and gulped with contented satisfaction. TallMan then offered the water to the others.

"The Navajo don't write with our alphabet," the Farmer explained.

"My mother," TallMan explained, "was a European. She was a sickly child captured from a Puritan preacher. Her child's name was Eunice. After years, her father found her, but then saw she had adapted to the tribal ways and even forgot English, so he surrendered his own daughter up to the tribe and he sent a missionary to teach the tribe English. I was raised with the values of my tribe and my Puritan grandfather," TallMan concluded.

"So, you lived in peace, then?" Button asked.

"Tribes fight, just as your countries fight. The only consistent peace was from following the laws of Doodaa-Tsaahi, which were difficult to follow, but with forgiveness, we found true freedom. Despite the turkey egg strife in my tribe, it all worked out to benefit my people.'

"Turkey egg?" Button asked.

"That's what he calls me," the farmer explained, "Because in the sun, I get dots on my face, like you see on the egg of the turkey."

"Freckles?" Button clarified.

"But, I also chose the public name of Farmer," Farmer explained. "It's understood by TallMan's tribe, as well as the Iroquois and Hurons."

"And," TallMan continued, "to resume with the story of my mother, she forgave the people who captured her and formed a bond with the family who took her in."

TallMan glanced up, then said, "She would tell me my grandmother, her adopted mother, had lost a child and hoped for another. My mother became that adopted child. Their kindness toward her opened the door for her to forgive her captors."

TallMan squinted to ascertain if he kept the attention of his small audience, "Her forgiveness then opened the door for learning about the European ways. Learning about the European ways meant I had to learn the European alphabet and speech, which I would never use for my own native tongue, but I was willing because of the example of my mother."

"And her kindness," Farmer added. "Her knowledge of the lands helped save the crops my family was in danger of losing in this place."

"Yes," TallMan agreed, "There are no words that use your f,p,q,r,v or x. I benefited from having a mother who had English beginnings. It allowed me to learn the medicine and languages of many European people."

"How easy would it be for me to learn your native tongue, TallMan," Button asked, "or of any tribe?"

TallMan replied, "Most tribes can master English because English has been taught by missionaries over the last century. The tribes, however, do not send out language teachers to your land. Besides, your people seem to have little interest in learning our ways and our language. Rather, they seem to have an interest in taking what we have built for generations." TallMan paused, "But, that is based on my personal observations of a few."

Button asked, "You have traded with some, and called them friend. You have fought against others, and called them foe. Yet, have you witnessed any true-good in people?"

TallMan thought for a long moment, "I have heard of the love of the Ojibwa."

"Ojibwa?" Button asked.

"But, I cannot tell you this story." TallMan cautioned.

"Pray, tell me why?" Button asked.

"Because it involves both the Ojibwa and one of your Colonies," TallMan crossed his arms firmly.

Button sat there looking at the Turkey

egg spotted faced farmer and then at the silent solid TallMan, who sat there unblinking.

"Tell me. I will not judge," Button stated.

TallMan uncrossed his arms. "I will tell you." He took a deep breath, "Over a decade ago, Chief Pontiac and sixty of his warriors agreed to have a peace talk with the English garrison at Detroit. It was around 1763."

Farmer interjected, "His plan, it was discovered later, was to feign a desire for peace with the colonies, but to plan for war. He was to give a signal to his Ojibwa warriors at the end of his peace negotiations speech."

"A signal?" Button asked.

"To slaughter all the LongCoats in your Fort Wayne of the Detroit tribe," TallMan clarified. "But, there was an Ojibwa maiden who had fallen in love with major Gladwyn, the commander at Fort Wayne.

She shared the Ojibwa Chief Pontiac's plan with Gladwyn. Chief Pontiac came to the peace council and gave his speech, but then Major Gladwyn gave Chief Pontiac a surprise..."

"Major Gladwyn," The Farmer added, "issued a call to arms to his soldiers before Chief Pontiac could signal his warriors to attack the fort. It surprised them all," the farmer slipped in.

"That chief," TallMan concluded, "pretended to want peace when he really wanted to slaughter all the Halgai Lagai-or... the white eyes. Because of the love of a woman, they were forced to complete the peace treaty."

"Fascinating" Button exclaimed, "To think the love of one woman changed history... prevented a slaughter of the fort."

TallMan leaned into Button, "Because my mother loved and forgave, her father let her go and gave our tribe English. Because of that, I speak and read

English better than most Englishmen. This knowledge allowed me to travel and learn healing from people of other nations, which is making my world a better place. Yes, the seed of love from one person can impact generations."

"Well," the farmer started as he reclined on his woven blanket, pulling another blanket over him for warmth, "In the morning, we can tell you why TallMan lives secretly in the forest... and how that may help you find out what really happened to your wife..."

And then he started to snore.

9 CHAPTER 56: (APRIL 1776) The Bang, the Footprints, the window, but what of the shot?

"I do believe we are making good progress, Witherspoon," Bryce stated. "We are here in the home of your employer, Mr. Hargreaves, creating a plausible hypothesis to explain how his murder was done. If we change Magistrate Pinkney's opinion, and convince him it was murder, I hope to enlist his help and actually catch the culprit. Justice must be meted out."

Bryce sat down in one of the chairs in Floyd Hargreaves' study while Witherspoon remained standing.

"Yes, sir," the butler, Witherspoon,

acknowledged. "We know how to erase foot prints. We know how to lock a window from the outside so it looks as if it were locked from the inside. So, we now can show that this ghost was really human. What we still do not know is, how could the sound of a shot be heard without a firearm?"

"Hmm. Yes, let us decipher how to shoot a firearm without an actual firearm and without being in the room at the time of the shot," Bryce started. "If the noise of a folded paper box was not loud enough to mimic a fire arm, then perhaps we need something stronger," Bryce suggested.

"Stronger, sir?" Witherspoon asked.

"Yes, Witherspoon," Bryce stated. "Have you gunpowder? We shall both untangle this ball of yarn, yet."

Witherspoon walked to a cabinet and extracted a leather pouch filled with gun powder.

"Floyd... Uh, Mr. Hargreaves kept gun powder in this study?" Bryce asked.

"Yes, sir," Witherspoon replied.

"Does he also keep a firearm here?" Bryce asked.

"I do not think so, Sir," Witherspoon replied. "The gunpowder was left by a visitor and Mr. Hargreaves wanted to have it set aside to return the gunpowder pouch to the gentleman, sir, when he returned. Mr. Hargreaves was not one for hunting, nor duels. He was a man of business, as you know."

After a long pause, Bryce Aiden Tyler, the former business partner of the deceased Floyd Hargreaves, asked, "Think back, Witherspoon, to that day. Then look around this room. Please tell me if you see anything out of place. Anything at all."

The devoted butler took his time and walked the perimeter of the room. Bryce stood up and followed Witherspoon around. Bryce would get out of his way as Witherspoon concentrated, making mental notes.

"I only notice, Sir," Witherspoon started, "if we look out the window, we see twigs on the branches close to the window are broken, but not cut off. When I trim the bushes, I trim the outside of the hedge away from the wall. The front of the bush seen from the walkway down there. I also trim the tops. I do not trim the inside by the wall more than once per year. And I see healthy leaves have fallen to the soil, twigs are torn and hanging, not cleanly clipped."

"So, can we assume that a person stood outside between the wall and the hedge?" Bryce asked.

"I think we can assume that, Sir," Witherspoon replied.

"So that was outside. What do you notice inside? " he quizzed the butler.

Witherspoon stretched out an arm and

pointed to a silver bowl underneath the window sill, "That bowl I had polished a few days ago. Mr. Hargreaves asked me to fill it with sweets to have with his tea. The sweets are gone, but now I see a dark smudge. The sweets would not have created such a mark. I would have to re-polish the bowl to remove that smudge."

Bryce picked up the bowl and examined it carefully, rubbing the discolored substance then smelling his fingers.

Bryce Aiden Tyler now focused on Witherspoon, then asked, "This window, Witherspoon? Does the sun ever stream in around tea time?"

"It does sir," Witherspoon replied. "I usually close the drapes to prevent the late morning sun from glaring in the room. If you are sitting where Mr. Hargreaves was found, the sun would glint in his eyes making it very difficult to read anything or even look up. But, now I see the drapes were open, and I had already closed them early in the morning. I knew Mr. Hargreaves wanted to spend the day in the room to permit me and Silversmith to go about our duties and Miss Jane's project."

"This smudge, Witherspoon, could be from a firearm igniting too close, but the angle is odd... I believe it is a gun powder burn, but..." Bryce shrugged, perplexed.

He took the leather pouch of gunpowder, which Witherspoon had found earlier. He poured a small amount of gun powder into the bowl, then placed the bowl by the window, in the sun.

"Now," Bryce surmised, "If our murderer used a match, then he would have had to light the match, place it upright in a pile of gunpowder, and get out the window before the match burned down, which does not leave very much time at all. No... and we do not have a burnt match stick anywhere that I can see..."

"So," Witherspoon commented, "the

gun powder had to be ignited without a match?"

"The murderer knew the gunpowder would be here, which means there is an accomplice who posed as a client and pretended to leave the gunpowder behind for the real murderer to use at a later date," Bryce commented.

"He was a new client," Witherspoon commented, "nor do I think he has returned since. I think he was from Ireland and fancied himself to be important. After he left, Mr. Hargreaves simply shook his head and did not seem impressed at all."

"So this client left the gun powder by accident, but really for another person to use it to pour into this bowl and create the false sound of a shot, but what would ignite it, if not a match?" Bryce thought out loud.

"Sir?" Witherspoon asked.

"Your employer's body was moved...

moved to this desk after he was shot. The assailant walked to the window, covering his footprints with some sort of chalk dust. He crawled out the window, and damaged your hedge in the process. But before he closed the window, he filled this dish with gun powder, but then he realized he was missing something... something to ignite it. Do you have a magnifying lens?" Bryce asked.

Witherspoon walked to the desk and extracted a large handled ornately framed magnifying lens, handing it to Bryce.

"This is beautiful work, but the edges are too ornate to allow it to stand up on its end... and remember we did not find a lens nor a matchstick... so..." Bryce spun around to Witherspoon, "He could not use this but something like it. Witherspoon, the murderer was about to leave the window and then realized he needed something to ignite the gunpowder and he had to use something he did not plan on using.

Something which could be propped up to catch the angle of the sun..." Bryce tapped his lip as he thought and looked for something to prop up the lens so it could catch the rays of the streaming sunshine.

The sun beam shaft traveled through the windowpane and hit the magnifying lens at the right angle.

Satisfied, Bryce ushered Witherspoon from the room and closed the door behind them. They both remained outside in the hallway near the doors of the study, awaiting the results of their experiment.

"Now, this is about the same time of day that you heard the shot, I believe. Let us be patient," Bryce urged.

"Is it possible, Sir..." Witherspoon started.

"Yes, my good man?" Bryce encouraged.

"Is it possible it was not a magnifying glass, but a smaller lens such as a monocle? And if the owner didn't have it on him, but then later did... after the sound of the shot, but before Magistrate Pinkney arrived?" the Butler's voice trailed off.

Suddenly, the gunpowder ignited with a bang. A very loud bang.

"Do you think that," Bryce asked Witherspoon, "...could have been what you heard through the door?"

Witherspoon replied, "Sir, do you think when we were trying to get into the room... when I assisted you when you removed the pins from the hinges... when Silversmith ran out to fetch the Magistrate Karl Pinkney and his brother and doctor... when Jane was trying to call to her Uncle... and..."

"...and when Mr. Tweedbottom said he would check for intruders outside and then returned a moment later..." Bryce added.

"He could have, Sir," Witherspoon added. "Perhaps used that as an excuse to hurry out back to retrieve his monocle."

Witherspoon cleared his throat as he mused, "Is it possible sir, that the monocle did not have to be inside? Perhaps whoever it was realized they forgot to ignite the gunpowder after the window had locked. Perhaps they had to set up something such as a monocle outside the window... or...perhaps using the twigs of the bush to prop it into the right position."

Witherspoon pointed, "The bowl was very close to the window, so would it have mattered if the lens was on the inside of the window or the outside?"

"We are not here to accuse an established tailor simply because he was here that day," Bryce mentioned.

"Indeed, Sir," Witherspoon agreed.

"But, if it was outside, it would explain

why your hedges were disturbed in such a manner... and why Mr. Tweedbottom volunteered to investigate and quickly returned, later to produce his monocle when ...as you say... he did not have it at tea earlier."

"Miss Jane," Witherspoon explained, "told me a day or so later that Mr. Tweedbottom had to borrow her lorgnette. Yet Silversmith saw Mr. Tweedbottom using his monocle only after the magistrate removed Karl Pinkney's body. So, why did he not use his monocle at tea? Why did he have to borrow Miss Jane's lorgnette?"

"But to convince Magistrate Karl Pinkney, whose salary is paid by the Crown, that one of the town's most vocal supporters of the Crown would have reason to kill Floyd Hargreaves... I mean, to me, Mr. Tweedbottom was about to ask Mr. Hargreaves for permission to take Jane's hand in marriage. He created a fashion for men to allow them to identify how loyal they are to the crown with the red on the cuff... I mean why would he kill Floyd Hargreaves? And if he did, how would I convince Magistrate Pinkney? How would I convince Jane? What if we are mistaken?"

"I do not know, Sir, but he could be a likely candidate based on what we have discovered thus far," Witherspoon commented.

"Witherspoon?" Bryce asked as his eyes narrowed, "Did your employer ever keep a journal of personal notes of some sort?"

10 CHAPTER 57: (MAY 1776)
Tweedbottom and Jane's Walk

Jane spoke softly with her strolling companion, Mr. Tweedbottom, as they walked the grounds of Sarah Wilson's estate, "I feel fortunate that the manner's hostess, Lady Sarah Wilson, is allowing me to stay on while my new friend resides with the Dunlaps. Those printers do not have enough room to take Silversmith and me together in..."

The moist dewy grass brushed against Jane's ankles, darkening the heels of her walking shoes. Tweedbottom looked as if he were trying to offer his arm for Jane to take. She did not comply and acted as if she did not notice his gesture. Jane was uncertain about the sort of message she should give Mr.Tweedbottom.

"I admit, I was taken aback when I first saw you, here at this estate, but..." Jane started as she glanced at Mr. Tweedbottom, "...there is something quite comforting in having you at my side."

"I am pleased I can be a comfort to you, Miss Hargreaves," Tweedbottom said softly.

"Oh, it is Jane, please... remember to call me Jane..." Jane smiled.

"You are fortunate indeed to have Lady Sarah Wilson view you as..." Mr. Tweedbottom mentioned, "...as a friend and open this palace to you... She is the caliber of people you should associate with... not those middling workers..."

Jane pondered Tweedbottom's comments for a moment. She knew Mr. Tweedbottom meant to isolate her from

Bryce Aiden Tyler, her Uncle's business partner, but she assumed Tweedbottom was jealous of Mr. Tyler as if he were a romantic rival, which of course, he was not.

But, then Jane recalled the incident in which a young woman burst into her chambers as Silversmith was dressing Jane for dinner at the estate. It was exactly then Silversmith and Jane had overheard the accusations tossed by this intruder, Eliza Lucas, that Lady Sarah Wilson was no lady at all. Miss Lucas had accused Sarah Wilson of being an untrustworthy trickster who had stolen the brooch belonging to Miss Lucas' mother... so why would Tweedbottom not know this about this very 'Lady Sarah Wilson' he encouraged Jane to befriend?

One other thing bothered Jane, while she inhaled the country air of Lady Sarah Wilson's estate as she silently walked beside Mr. Tweedbottom... It was the sort of company invited to Lady Sarah's dinners. Luckily, Silversmith had asked about the other guests and discovered a very different truth than the façade presented to Jane at dinner. Each guest had some sort of sordid history. These were the types of friends Jane's Uncle Floyd would have warned her against, yet Tweedbottom was pushing her toward these people.

Was Tweedbottom trying to get her out of the way, keep her from returning to her home, or was Tweedbottom genuinely enamored by the image Lady Sarah Wilson was presenting?

"What thoughts occupy your pretty mind, my dear?" Tweedbottom asked the silent Jane.

"Thoughts? Oh..." Jane stuttered, "Oh. Um. I was thinking about the lovely ladies which the Lady of the house entertains... and it made me wonder of the men she invited."

"The men?" Tweedbottom stopped walking. They were near the front of the estate, by the gravel path where the carriages would drop off and pick up passengers.

"Well," Jane started, "None of them seem to wear your creations that I could recognize. I assumed they would be proud wardrobe collectors of your tailor shop creations."

"One must attend parties, Jane, to obtain contacts..." Tweedbottom started, "The men are prospective possible customers..."

"I see," Jane said, her thoughts wandering.

Mr. Tweedbottom stopped and faced Jane by stepping in front of her, "I only resolved to attend this event after I saw that you had decided to take your Uncle Floyd's place and attend the operatic performance. I hired the swiftest carriage in hopes of arriving in time..."

"In time? For business opportunity with the opera singer? Or to see me? How did you know I was attending when I did not R.S.V.P.? Shall I assume you were acquainted with members of the household prior to my visit?"

Frustrated, Tweedbottom, barked, "Women do not understand the nuances of business. Jane! Yes! It is better to conduct business around a refined Irish Opera singer instead of a banjo performance," Tweedbottom's face turned red, "Which as you know may promote dancing!"

"Dancing?" Jane was now fully engaged in the conversation. "You object to dancing, yet create fabulous gowns for balls? What of the waltz?" Jane protested, "I know several dances, the waltz is simply one of them. Does knowing the waltz make me a wanton woman, Mr. Tweedbottom?"

Abruptly, Mr. Tweedbottom became quite calm and spoke very softly and slowly, "You digress, my dear Jane." He started, "I understand your recent tragedy has vexed you, making you unable to see reality. I feel it is best for you to remain here and avoid returning to your Uncle's home, a house of tragedy."

"I would thank you, Mr. Tweedbottom, for not calling the home which has sheltered Silversmith and me a house of tragedy." Jane's jaw clenched.

In the same slow deliberate tones, Mr. Tweedbottom said, "I feel so lucky that I was at your side to comfort you during the horrific incident of your Uncle's self-murder." Tweedbottom boldly outstretched his arm to gently embrace Jane about her waist. When she looked at his hand placed on her waist, then looked at him with a scowl, he immediately removed his hand, acting as if he were stretching, instead.

"Yes," Jane agreed, "I consider myself fortunate that you, my dear friend, was at tea during the incident so that I might seek solace and comfort in your company. It would have been dreadful to have shouldered the news alone." Jane smiled, leaning a shoulder toward Tweedbottom playfully.

She realized she had been harsh with Mr. Tweedbottom and in her thoughts she told herself that she should welcome Tweedbottom's advances. After all, who else was there to be a suitor at her age?

"Let us not argue, my dear Jane," Tweedbottom's voice became husky. "Let us realize that when one quarrels, our hearts race and we should be free to release our passions."

Jane looked at the ground. "You may think this silly, but I wrote a poem," and Jane smiled as she pulled out a tiny folded paper.

"You wrote something for me?" Tweedbottom was genuinely touched as he reached out his hand.

Jane handed the paper to him. He unfolded it, then patted his pocket for his monocle, raised one eyebrow to insert the lens, and then read the note.

"Your fashion sense is divine; your friendship is mine; betwixt heaven and earth my heart doth resign."

Tweedbottom read aloud with moisture welling up in his glassy eyes, then whispered, "Oh, Jane. The prose is a bit awkward. Pedantic, even. But you attempted a rhyme about our friendship and I think that is wondrous progress. Is it not liberating to embrace the fact that we are never too old..."

"Too old?" Jane echoed.

"Never too old to hire an English tutor, are we?" Tweedbottom winked as he kissed the paper, and slipped it into his pocket.

"Well, not quite the reaction I thought it might elicit," Jane muttered under her breath, then brightly said with a forced grin, "I imagine, Mr. Tweedbottom, that you intended that to be a kind response."

Just then, Silversmith came running toward them, calling, "Miss Jane? Miss Jane!" She approached breathlessly, "It's time to dress for dinner, Miss."

"Oh, is that all?" Mr. Tweedbottom sighed relief, "I thought something urgent was afoot." He laughed to himself. "I leave you in Silversmith's capable hands. I understand women and know it takes an enormous amount of time to prepare to dress..." Tweedbottom stated as he crisply bowed while returning his monocle to a tiny pocket sewn just for that item. He tapped another pocket, which now contained Jane's poem, turned on his heels, and left.

Jane stood there observing Mr. Tweedbottom walk away.

Silversmith lowered her voice, "I was watching at the window as you asked me to, Miss Jane. I came out as soon as I saw you hand him the paper."

"Well done, Silversmith..." Jane started, "Well done."

Silversmith asked, "Before we walk back into the house, where everything can be heard, tell me, Miss Jane, did he need his monocle to read the note?"

"Indeed, Silversmith. He did..." Jane stroked the chain around her neck. She played with the lorgnette at the end of the chain, then she observed, "Witherspoon and Mr. Tyler were correct. Please reply to their letter explaining our test and the results. I cannot write a letter, because I am sure it will be read. You must communicate with them in secret when you are away from the estate. I shall give you money to have it delivered."

"Aye, Miss Jane. I can mail a response next time I run an errand for you," Silversmith concurred.

Jane turned to Silversmith, "However, proving he has poor eyesight does not mean he was involved in Uncle Floyd's death. It only proves that he always reaches for that tiny pocket when he needs to read something."

"But," Silversmith prodded, "you said that Mr. Tweedbottom had to borrow your lorgnette at tea because he did not have his monocle. And you also told me

Mr. Tweedbottom had his monocle to read the invitation to this place after the magistrate left. I told Witherspoon what you had said, which is why he wrote back to suggest we test Mr. Tweedbottom's dependence upon that monocle. He does indeed always have it with him. It is odd, me thinks, that he has a tiny pocket sewn into all his waistcoats, yet did not have his monocle at tea time before we found your Uncle."

"I don't want to create suspicions when I also must think about the future... and I must return home to examine the accounts, but I do not think my allowance is enough to support Uncle's household. I must be realistic, Silversmith, for both our sakes, to provide us both shelter. Perhaps it was self-murder after all, and I'm feeding fanciful stories to myself..." Jane sighed, "Perhaps I'm being unfair to Mr.Tweedbottom. He is not romantic, and unpleasantly harsh at times, but..."

"God gives us all instincts," Silversmith commented. "I'd listen to them. I wouldn't fret over trying to support a household when you haven't even returned home yet to evaluate the state of affairs. God can see more solutions than we can."

"I just don't want to become a bitter old spinster who thinks ill of everyone around her," Jane explained. "Mr. Tweedbottom was at my side when I heard the bang, so he surely couldn't have had anything to do with what happened to Uncle Floyd. Mr. Tweedbottom thinks it's self-murder... and he is showing me attentions which would indicate he would take care of us both... Accept reality... I must accept reality..."

As Silversmith and Jane stood at the entrance to Sarah Wilson's mansion, Jane suddenly stopped and turned to Silversmith.

"Silversmith," Jane started, "you have been in my employ for many years, now."

"Yes, Miss." Silversmith concurred.

"Have your duties become too routine or boring. Do you feel challenged?" Jane asked.

"I'm not quite sure how to answer that, Miss. I think I do a good job considering things have not been easy these last few months..." Silversmith replied, "Why do you ask?"

Jane looked up, then back at Silversmith. "Something Polly Mulhoolin said to me in the carriage while waiting for you and Billy Dawes to butcher the wild boar meat on the side of the road." Jane took a deep breath, "Silversmith, I am going to issue you a challenge. A mission, if you will."

"A mission, Miss Jane?" Silversmith's voice cracked with bewilderment.

"Yes," Jane was quite determined, now. "I want you and the driver Billy Dawes to go to a place. I shall give you money... a lot of it... so I will be trusting you to do your best. This is a secret mission. If anybody asks you where you are going, tell them that I said, 'Silversmith, I want you to return home.'"

"And do you want me to return home, Miss Jane?" Silversmith asked, "And have Mr. Dawes drive me, leaving you here without a carriage?"

"No..." Jane said simply as she leaned toward Silversmith, whispering to avoid any possible curious eavesdroppers.

Then Jane explained the idea she had, which had just popped into her head.

11 CHAPTER 58: (MARCH 1776)
Farmer and The Indian Secret

The next morning, TallMan, Farmer, and Button awoke inside the hollowed out tree cave.

Button recalled Farmer's last words were that he would explain why TallMan was here and how that might help Button find his wife. It seemed illogical, but he was curious and wanted to hear the predicament of the Farmer who looked like a turkey egg, and the raven haired Indian hosting him.

"The king's militia feel it is their right to take, even when it is not theirs," Farmer explained as he awoke.

"This does not concern me," Button responded. "When I came to this country, I worked in the Georgia colony and then moved when my Irish wife fulfilled her indentured contract. We planned to live off the land. To be left in peace."

"If any nation comes to our land," TallMan sat up and said... "makes an agreement with anybody, then breaks it with that person, it means he will eventually break it with you. That one has proven they cannot be trusted." He sighed as he turned to Button, "It's a matter of time before your cabin or your neighbor's home is attacked, again. Today you are a victim. Tomorrow, become a warrior to combat this evil."

"How," Button laughed, "am I to change the fact that my wife and I were victims of an attack?"

"You cannot dwell on your attackers. You must discover who hired them," TallMan shot back.

Button replied, "Hired them? I believe those Indians were going to be paid by a slave trader once they delivered me. They were not hired by anybody."

"The attack on your home is part of a larger scheme," TallMan replied.

"What?" Button said, surprised.

The Farmer nodded, "TallMan just told me on my last visit that back in 1770 in just the colony of Virginia, ten percent of colonists were slaves. Today in 1776, its forty percent."

"Think," TallMan interjected, "about 200,000 enslaved in just that township. In New Amsterdam... or New York, however you call it, that is 26,000 slaves or fourteen percent of the people there. This includes people who came from Ireland, from Spain from Portugal and other lands."

"New colonists became slaves?"

Farmer nodded, "Some were brought here to be slaves. Others came here to be settlers, and have been kidnapped to be slaves... as what almost happened to you and your Irish wife."

Button sat very still, then protested, "I do not control the laws of any colony. This subject does not concern me!"

"And what of Connecticut?" TallMan persisted. "15,000 or eight percent. What of Rhode Island, 3,000 or six percent? You can break it up by colony or take it as a whole. I estimate nearly a quarter of a million people in all your colonies are enslaved against their will... just as your own Crown tried to kidnap you and enslave you."

"What?" Button exclaimed. "I was kidnapped by men like you, TallMan. Indians. Not the British."

"Your British men of business," TallMan corrected, "Your British crown, purchases slaves of all races." He took a deep breath. "To further insult my people," TallMan stated, "they hire rebels from all our tribes to do the kidnapping, so your British businessmen need not be so close to the actual act... and to cause residents in the colonies to fear Indians so they do not suspect their own neighbors, who are behind this scheme."

Button was speechless. He placed both his elbows on his crossed legs as he sat and rested his chin on the palms of his hands, staring blankly at nothing in particular.

"So," Button spoke, softly, slowly, "the slave trade is so profitable that they are not limiting themselves to distant exotic lands and the Irish... They are taking anybody they can overpower... like me. They are acting indiscriminately all to secure free labor to increase their profits?"

"Exactly," TallMan exclaimed, "and they are blaming many tribes for the kidnapping of colonists, which the crown hires the Indians to do."

The Farmer looked at Button, "If you share your story at the meeting town, as a man who actually escaped one of these attacks, perhaps it will encourage those with power to write to the King and ask him to stop."

"You want me," Button asked, "To help somebody write a letter to the King?"

"No," TallMan explained, "A man, Robert Livingston, will scribe a letter. We hope that letter will compel the crown to cease slave raids... among other things... for... hopefully... five years."

"Mr. Livingston," the Farmer started, "has not been able to draft a compelling letter. I believe what happened to you could clarify Mr. Livingston's thoughts so he may complete his letter."

"Mr. Livingston," TallMan explained, "needs to complete the document, get it to Manhattan where King George III has set up in the plaza, an immense statue of himself, covered in glittering gold. Clearly, your King George intends to become king of this land. Our land."

"How does any of this get me closer to finding out if my wife lives or not?" Button asked.

"You help us, and we'll help you inquire for your bride," Farmer shrugged.

"You led me to believe you had specific information regarding my wife," Button snapped at Farmer, "which you would share if I listened to your mission. Well, I have listened and I do not know anything new about the welfare of my wife."

"If you come to the Meeting Town and help me serve water," Farmer proposed, "and tell your story in order to inspire Mr. Livingston to complete the letter to the King, then..."

The farmer leaned in and enunciated carefully, "perhaps we can successfully ask the officials if they have heard about your wife. They should know more than a simple farmer, such as me. I do wish to provide information regarding the welfare of your wife, however I do not currently possess it...but I know to whom you may speak to get it..."

Farmer straightened up proudly and asked, "So, now will you serve water there?"

"Will you go?" TallMan asked Button.

12 CHAPTER 59: (APRIL 1776) Floyd Hargreaves Had a Journal?

Witherspoon got up to answer the front door of the Hargreaves residence, hesitating as he passed the study door where his deceased employer, Floyd Hargreaves, had died. The knocking was loud and persistent. Bryce Aiden Tyler, Floyd's former business partner, followed close behind the butler.

"I'm sure we are on to something, Witherspoon," Bryce repeated as he looked down at his own feet while he followed Witherspoon to the front door.

"I do not recall, Sir," Witherspoon replied, "If Mr. Hargreaves had a journal which he hid. I may have seen him take notes in a small leather bound book, but I cannot recall where he could have kept that book..."

Witherspoon arrived at the door. "It is logical," he started before he opened the door, "that if there was a notebook, it would be in the room where Mr. Hargreaves died, but I would have to search for it."

"Very well, Witherspoon," Bryce Aiden replied, "After whoever is at the door leaves, we can search for it."

"And," Witherspoon added, "If I do find something, perhaps I should send word to Silversmith."

"Oh, yes. Absolutely..." Bryce Aiden concurred, "It would be too forward at this time for me to write to Jane. I fear she thinks ill of me for some reason... and it is not appropriate for me to write to Silversmith. Yes. Witherspoon, you must continue to be the mode of communication between us until that fellow you found, that..."

"Billy Dawes, sir, the carriage driver," Witherspoon added as the door knocker was rapidly struck again impatiently.

"Until Mr. Dawes drives Silversmith and Miss Hargreaves home. Then, I can perhaps explain... what... well... I mean, our discoveries to confirm Miss Hargreaves' suspicion that perhaps her uncle Floyd did not commit self-murder... and... and... answer the door, Witherspoon..." Bryce Aiden stepped back a few steps as Witherspoon opened the door.

On the other side of the door stood Magistrate Karl Pinkney, and his brother.

"Good day, Witherspoon," Magistrate Karl Pinkney started, "May I see Miss Jane Hargreaves, please."

Witherspoon replied to both Magistrate Karl Pinkney and his brother, who stood silently, "I'm afraid Miss Hargreaves is not at home, gentlemen. Would you like to leave your card or a message?"

Magistrate Pinkney looked in past Witherspoon and saw Bryce Aiden Tyler. He stepped in, uninvited. His brother followed. Witherspoon and Bryce Aiden Tyler looked at each other as Witherspoon closed the door behind them.

The group remained standing in the foyer.

"My brother and I have come to collect the fee for taking away Miss Hargreaves's uncle's body. There are costs involved," Magistrate Karl Pinkney explained.

Bryce Aiden spoke up. "Good day, Magistrate," Bryce Aiden Tyler said to Magistrate Pinkney and then to his brother, "Sir. Good day to you, as well." After the nods of acknowledgement, Bryce Aiden asked, "Since Miss Hargreaves is unavailable for the nonce, might I inquire as to how much Miss Hargreaves owes the Crown?"

The magistrate's brother looked at the magistrate and with his nod of approval, handed an official paper to Bryce Aiden Tyler. He looked at it with some surprise as to the amount, but then said, "I see. A goodly sum, it is. However, I believe I have the funds to clear this debt. May I pay to clear Jane Hargreaves of this debt?"

After some discussion with his brother, Magistrate Karl Pinkney replied, "You'll have to give the money to my brother, here."

Bryce Aiden nodded and reached into his pocket to extract a small pouch and produced the coins needed to satisfy this debt.

"Thank you, Mr. Tyler," the magistrate's brother said as he took Bryce Aiden's money. "This will help me greatly being paid so promptly."

"Help you?" Bryce Aiden asked confused. He looked at Witherspoon's flat expression and realized the butler also didn't understand the comment.

13 CHAPTER 60: (JUNE 1776) Secret Barn Meeting- Three Months After The Raid

"Opposite me... Across the room," Farmer pointed away to where Button should stand, then pointed to jugs of water they had brought on the cart, and said, "Goblets stay full for any gent talking." The secret meeting was just setting up.

It was bright outside, but one wouldn't know it with the barn doors closed. The stable hands had just finished cleaning the stables to prepare for these visitors. They took the horses out to pasture, but would only be gone until nightfall. That gave the attendees of the secret meeting a little over an hour... maybe two... but if the weather turned foul, then the stable boys would need to return to the barn early.

Button replied to the Farmer, "Why have they changed the meeting from the old location to this new barn? "

Farmer replied, "The red coats know the other place, don't they. They don't know this place... not yet..."

"I'm not seeing much getting accomplished in these meetings, Farmer," Button started. "I appreciate you taking me to all these various gatherings, but I think after this one, I'll be heading on my way..."

"You're cabin's been raided," Farmer drawled, concerned.

"I know, I know I cannot return. I don't know if my wife has survived... but I must start rebuilding my life and I'm not one to get involved in what you and

TallMan find so... so... intriguing."

"Ben Franklin's expected to show to this one..." Farmer tempted.

Button shook his head as if that didn't matter

"And somebody from Ireland. A singer..." Farmer went on.

Button explained, "I'm rather concerned I've overstayed my welcome with you... and I must get on with my life. Even though I cannot ever live in that cabin, again... well, I'd have to rebuild it... exhausting prospect. But..., I should go back to ask if there is any word of my wife. If there is no knowledge of her whereabouts, then I must accept that she is dead and perhaps... I don't know... I'll return to Georgia and see if I can get rehired there. Building a home in the middle of nowhere is not... It is just not for... for me... it was my wife's dream... and it's meaningless without her..." Button lamented.

Farmer said, "Working the farm's been easier with your help. Stay."

Button picked up a jug and started to walk to the other side of the barn. "Doing this, filling goblets with water... no matter how fresh and sweet, is pointless. I mean, I understand most attendees cannot bring their own servants. I am aware the attendees cannot risk the gossiping of the servants," Button went on, "So, yes, the position of filling water and guarding secrets is important, but I cannot live out the rest of my days this way."

"It's helpful," Farmer encouraged.

Button looked up and then down at his feet before replying. Then he looked at Farmer and said, "I am following you from one clandestine meeting to the next in hopes I'll meet somebody who might know who raided my home. I don't care about these political issues which concern them. I have not met anybody who can help me ascertain where my wife is. Nobody has been able to say if she's alive or not, and if it is at all safe to return to my cabin. Everybody has troubling problems to occupy their thoughts. You don't need me for this water task... if anything I've gotten underfoot." Button extended a hand to Farmer. "I thank you, Farmer, for putting me up for the last few weeks... or has it been months? Anyway, I appreciate your cause. I appreciate what TallMan is trying to do and that, as an Indian, he cannot come to these meetings. I will simply support both your goals of peace and freedom from a distance with my positive hopes..."

"But... About to start..." Farmer reminded.

"I will stay to clean up after the meeting disbands. Then, I will take my leave in the morning," Button reassured.

"But, Ben Franklin..." Farmer pleaded. He pointed as the great ambassador had just entered the barn and looked for somewhere to sit. "The singer..." Farmer pointed to another very well dressed man, then looked at Button.

"It doesn't matter who attends this meeting," Button explained. Then, with jug in hand, he walked over to Benjamin Franklin and filled his goblet with water. Then, Button leaned up against the wall to keep an eye out for other attendees, man or woman, who would need to quench their thirst.

Button sighed. Why did progress seem so very slow. He thought of the horses grazing in verdant pastures. He recalled TallMan saying he could never attend these meetings himself because his Indian appearance had intimidated many, and he felt that negative gossip had discouraged people from even listening to him.

TallMan was not one for crowds. Button sighed, again.

He desperately missed Polly.

He wondered if the raid had not happened, would he have delivered his own baby girl? Or boy? Or twins? Well, maybe he will find out when he meets them in heaven.

14 What Just Happened?

Bryce Aiden Tyler and his manservant Witherspoon continue to hypothesize how the murder was done. They are convinced this was not a suicide.

Meanwhile Jane and Polly must contend with their own daily issues.

Will Bryce and Witherspoon find the answers to a murder in a child's game?

Will Button find the answers he seeks?

.

15 Did You Know...

When people say "El Dorado" it implies a location of fantastic wealth and possible opportunity which you could not take advantage of in your current location.

The characters in the *Firebrand* series mention Francisco Vasquez Coronado's determined hunt for El Dorado to obtain gold. (Chapter 6 of this book, continuous chapter 53 in the Firebrand saga.)

Coronado placed high value on the physical metal gold. This was not what the Zuni people had valued. A great treasure to one man may not be worth anything to another man.

Coronado's obsession skewed his ability to reason. He was determined to find something which was never there to begin with. His hunt was futile. Coronado had allowed his obsession, greed, and assumptions resulted in tragedy.

Coronado thought his social status would be elevated and he would be treated better. He assumed he would be adored and admired if only he could obtain this elusive gold. He allowed his delusion to twist him into an unreasonable man, whose tantrums resulted in the death of many, and scarred the lands in his search for something which never existed.

The first use of "El Dorado" (Spanish for "gilded one") may have been as early as 1596. The Spanish adventurers heard rumors about a king in the Amazon who dusted himself with gold dust. Rumors had it that this king was showered with jewels and gold by his own subjects as he strode along streets also paved with gold. Supposedly, this king was unaware of the value of these common gilded paving stones. This "gold bedecked king" story was so intriguing that the story circulated rapidly.

The lust for gold and power seems to never be satisfied. If you seek a little, you may thirst for more. The question becomes what morals will you compromise to get it and try to satisfy your insatiable desires? Would you harm another person? Take their life? Destroy the lands people live on? Falsely accuse another? Send a man to be executed? Know that a place of immeasurable riches which only you can take and claim as your own simply does not exist.

Initial stories of a tribe in South America living in a remote part of the Andes mountains (Columbia) may have started when a tribesman had a ceremony to take the throne. This was a tribe which may have believed in a deity who lived underwater, and that may have spun the tale of a man covered in gold who had so much he would toss it to the waters without a second thought.

In 1617 Sir Walter Raleigh made two trips to Guiana with his son, Watt, to search for this elusive El Dorado. Watt Raleigh was killed in a battle with Spaniards and the expedition was a disaster.

Eric Klingelhofer, an archaeologist at Mercer University in Macon, Georgia tried to find the Raleigh base camp. He was told that Walter was furious when he heard of his son's death and accused and blamed the survivor of the battle of carelessly letting his son die. The accused survivor killed himself in his ship cabin. Sir Walter Raleigh returned to England where King James had him beheaded for disobeying orders to avoid all fights with the Spanish.

So, Raleigh's lust for gold and power resulted in his own son's death, the deaths of many who accompanied him, and his own death. In addition he jeopardized international relations which could have caused the death of countless innocent citizens in a needless war.

Think twice before you hotly pursue treasure for the sake of treasure because you may lose far more than you could ever gain.

There are real cities named El Dorado. Below is a partial list. The spelling is both with and without a space

- ✓ El Dorado , KS 67042
- ✓ El Dorado , AR 71730
- ✓ El Dorado , CA 95623
- ✓ El Dorado Hills, CA 95630
- ✓ El Dorado Hills, CA 95762
- ✓ Eldorado Springs, CO 80025
- ✓ El Dorado Spring, MO 64744
- ✓ Eldorado, OH 45321
- ✓ Eldorado, IA 52175
- ✓ Eldorado, WI 54932
- ✓ Eldorado, IL 62930
- ✓ Eldorado, OK 73537
- ✓ Eldorado, TX 76936
- ✓ Dorado, PR 646

16 Vocabulary

In the early 1770s, before the colonies united into the United States of America, some words and terms were used, which may be explained in this section.

***Attribute* :** A quality or description of someone or something.

Drawing room: A room in a house where visitors may be entertained.

Epiphany: A moment when you suddenly feel that you understand. (The first recognition of Christ by the gentiles.)

Feign To pretend, or to act in a way you do not feel

Gauche: To lack social grace. To be crude, clumsy, awkward.

ABOUT Wynter Sommers

Wynter Sommers is the pseudonym for an American writing team, which harnesses multiple skills in technology, research, history and education. Formally trained with a PhD in Education, Wynter Sommers blends academic classroom experience, with corporate sophistication, and a passion for developing more effective student insights through engaging storytelling.

Wynter Sommers has a heart to inspire creativity and develop critical thinking skills, all to encourage readers to make wise choices in life.

Wynter Sommers takes each story and weaves the plot with classic gripping elements, which endure throughout repeated readings, revealing new meanings each time the story is explored. The small choices a reader makes in real life could have a lasting effect in future generations. This set of stories shows the origin of not just Bjorn Esterday and Sarah Paradise, but of their ancestors and the sort of world which was established, which unfolded in each generation until Bjorn and Sarah met.

It is rewarding to learn of heartfelt, thought provoking conversations taking place globally about the characters of these books. Should the reader be presented with extraordinary circumstances, it is the sincerest wish that they act with honor, truth and integrity to overcome obstacles in real life whilst the reader hones skills of self-reliance and collaborative teamwork despite barriers outside of the reader's control. Wynter Sommers hopes you enjoy the other *Bjorn Esterday Was not Born Yesterday* stories in this series.

www.ingramcontent.com/pod-product-compliance
Lightning Source LLC
Chambersburg PA
CBHW030035030726
47500CB00001B/124